BE THE BEST

AN INSPIRATIONAL BOOK FOR YOUNG RUGBY PLAYERS

CONTENTS

CHAPTER 1:   RUGBY...WHAT'S IT ALL ABOUT   PAGE 4

CHAPTER 2:   RUGBY...GIVING IT YOUR ALL   PAGE 14

CHAPTER 3:   RUGBY...YOUR FITNESS   PAGE 36

CHAPTER 4:   RUGBY...THE TEAM   PAGE 54

CHAPTER 5:   RUGBY...IN SCHOOLS.   PAGE 68

CHAPTER 6:   RUGBY...GETTING SELECTED   PAGE 72

CHAPTER 7:   RUGBY...THE NEXT STEP   PAGE 84

<u>Be inspired...</u>

I hope this book helps you become the best rugby player you can be. Rugby is such a fun and challenging sport to be involved in and I hope this book helps you in whatever stage of rugby you are at: whether it's at a local club, primary school or at regional level. I have coached many talented boys and girls over the years and I love seeing the enthusiasm young players have in today's game.

This book unites players from every age and every nation. You can learn from rugby union, rugby league and sevens...we all share a passion for the oval ball. Please draw inspiration from the words of great players such as Jason Critchley, Peter Elder, Shelley Rae and Jason Golden. Every professional player has had challenges they had to overcome to get where they are today so please don't give up when you face problems. Everyone has to spend some time on the sub bench, or deal with losing at some point.

Professional players from all over the world have contributed to this book and they want you to feel inspired and do well. This is the first time many of them have discussed the difficulties they faced as young players, from getting injured to not getting picked at trials.

Use this book as a handbook, personalise it and make it yours, highlight things that are important to you, fill in the charts, complete the challenges and have your questions answered by the Coachdoctor. Turn up to training and give 110%, listen to your coaches and work as a team. Push yourself and learn all you can from the people around you. If you want to succeed you will do. You have what it takes to be a world class player.

Good Luck,

Sarah Oliver

Chapter 1:

Rugby.... What's it all about?

This isn't your average book on rugby so I'm not going to talk about the ins and outs of rugby union, rugby league and seven's. If I did this book would be hundreds of pages long and after reading it you'd be no closer to being a better rugby player than you are now. You didn't pick up this book to see an illustrated guide to rugby through the ages....only retired players who are too old to play read things like that. No, you want something practical, something that will give you the edge. Something that will help you get where you want to be.

The question in the chapter's title isn't going to be answered here by me. No. It's going to be answered by you. What does rugby mean to you? You're the most important player in this book so it's time you started working. Fill in the box below by writing three things that rugby means to you. What is it about rugby that you love?

WHAT RUGBY MEANS TO ME

1.

2.

3.

Rugby unites

Rugby means a lot to people all across the world. Everyone has different reasons for loving rugby but every reason is valid. You might prefer rugby union or you might prefer rugby league. It doesn't matter. In this book every chapter is relevant to whichever code you play. Try and read everything and learn from every player. Don't skip players just because they play for the other code, they might have great tips that can improve your game. There have been some great rugby players who have played both types of rugby....in the future you could become one of them.

<u>Who plays rugby?</u>

Did you know that rugby is the second most popular sport in the world? Rugby is played in over 110 countries.

One reason why rugby is so popular is because it's a family sport. Everyone can play it and everyone can enjoy it. Dads can play, mums can play, boys can play, girls can play. You can have so much fun as a whole family just practicing it. You can play if you are tall, if you are small, if you are slim or if you are large. Size doesn't matter. There is a perfect position and team out there for everyone.

Now if you've been playing by the rules you should have listed what rugby means to you on the previous page. If you haven't you need to go back and fill it out. No cheating. If you want to be the best then you've got to listen to your coaches. You need to treat this book as a coach and do as it says....or else!

<u>What does rugby mean to players all around the world?</u>

Every player has different reasons for playing rugby. Every player loves rugby in a different way. Next time you are with your friends why not ask them what they love about rugby the most.

"I love everything about the game. I love learning how to play in different positions and playing matches. I love being part of a team."

Claire Park, England.

"I love the atmosphere after a match. I like chatting to the opposition players and having a laugh."

Peter McIntee, England.

"I love rugby because you have to use your mind and your body. You learn a lot about yourself and your team mates. And you get to tackle people!"

Vladimir Scott, United States.

"I love rugby because it doesn't matter if you're a bit chubby, or if you aren't the best at running."

Gemma Williams, Scotland.

"The part I most like about rugby is part of being a team, and the feeling you get when you all work as one and beat the other team mentally and physically on the pitch."

Edward Lewis, England.

"I love making big hits. There's nothing better than tackling someone hard."

Tom Dugarin, Wales.

"The things I love most about rugby are making friends and having fun."

Robyn Walls, England.

"I love the thrill of playing as a team, the energy and the pace of the game."

Alasdair Muller, England.

"Rugby is the best team sport I have ever played. I played football and soccer and nothing compares to the pain and joy you get from playing rugby. Rugby is the best team sport ever."

Steven Shenkman, Canada.

"The international rugby family. If you have your boots anywhere in the world you will be able to get a game on a Saturday!"

Max Malkin, England.

"I love the fact that anyone can play rugby, any shape, any size, because all positions require different skills. I love the fact that it's simple: if you want the ball, go and get it."

Shelley Rae, England.

Now you have read what players across the world love about rugby try and find all the words in the wordsearch below. All the words are taken from the player quotes.

WHAT WE LOVE ABOUT RUGBY WORDSEARCH

U	B	R	F	R	I	E	N	D	S
S	S	Y	U	W	A	L	E	S	B
A	C	A	N	A	D	A	L	T	C
Y	K	R	O	W	M	A	E	T	F
D	M	B	Y	L	I	M	A	F	C
O	T	I	M	A	T	C	H	B	O
B	I	N	E	N	G	L	A	N	D
E	H	D	N	A	L	T	O	C	S

FRIENDS   TEAMWORK   MATCH   USA
FAMILY   CANADA   WALES   HIT
SCOTLAND   ENGLAND   BODY   FUN

Everyone has a rugby story however old or young they are. Everyone can remember how they started playing and what it felt like to score their first try or win their first tournament. It might be that you've only just started playing so you haven't done these things yet so it might be easier to look at this page at a later date.

Have a read of Adam Geoghegan's rugby story and start thinking about your own rugby story as you go.

"I started playing rugby when I joined secondary school. I went to my first Devon county trial when I was fourteen. I played for Devon for the next four years with my friend from school. I also played for Plymstock RFC. I met my best friend Miles there.

Plymstock RFC did not have a colts team, so at the age of 16 I joined OPM'S newly formed colts team. We didn't win a game for the entire year. We didn't quit and join another team, instead me and Miles kept trying our best. We dragged our team along, and put everything we could into making it better. The next season we came 3rd in the league. Lots of important people in the club thanked us, but me and Miles both knew it takes everyone on the field to do their jobs, and it's a team effort.

In my last year of school, I was voted captain. At the same time, my best friend Miles, had been voted captain for his school. My team won most matches but in the final game of the season we were going to play Mile's team. I put on extra training sessions, and had my boys working harder than ever before.

On match day, there was very large crowd watching the game. It was only when our coach pointed out to me, with the line, "You know there here to watch you and Miles" that I realised how important the match was to both schools. It was no longer about the league, it was about pride.

We lost the match, by two points. It was described as an epic battle. I had broken a finger, cut open my head and had my ankle strapped. Miles was in a similar state. After the game, we went back to being best of friends. I don't think you get this in any other sport. It was hard to lose, especially to him, and I knew my team didn't like it either. Next year after I left the school, the first 15 beat Mile's old school twice in one season. They told me they did it for me. This meant more to me than any other award or winning a final, I had earned the respect of the people I was playing with. And even though I wasn't playing with them any more they were still running out onto that field for me, and trying to regain the pride I lost last year.

I am now 19, playing for OPM's mens first team. Last year we came 3rd in the Devon 1 league. Next year our aim is to win it. This is my rugby story to date.

Now it's time to write your rugby story down. It really is the beginning of your story because you are going to have many more years playing rugby. Who knows where you'll be when you finish. Professional players write their rugby stories and they get made into books called autobiographies.

MY RUGBY STORY

I STARTED PLAYING WHEN I WAS .... YEARS OLD.

THE FIRST TEAM I PLAYED FOR WAS ....

I PLAYED MY FIRST MATCH AGAINST ....

THE SCORE WAS .... WE WON/ LOST/ DREW.

IT WAS A SUNNY/ WINDY/ RAINY DAY.

MY BEST FRIEND AT RUGBY IS ....

MY FAVOURITE MATCH WAS AGAINST ....

I LOVED THAT MATCH BECAUSE..

....

....

....

MY FIRST TRY WAS ....

....

....

THE TOUGHEST MATCH I'VE PLAYED WAS ....

....

NEXT SEASON I WANT TO ....

My first match

We won the Scottish Festival !!!!

Making a scrapbook

Your rugby story is unique to you and it is very special even if you don't think so now. In years to come you will look back and try and remember what it was like. Sadly, many players forget to keep a record as they go and lots of good victories and happy memories are forgotten.

You can stop this happening by starting a scrapbook to record all your rugby moments. You should cut out your teams newspaper reports and keep tournament programmes and certificates in there. It's totally up to you what the scrapbook looks like. You can add anything you want. It's a great way to show grandparents what you've been up to and the can even help you collect things for it. Ask your parents to take a camera to big matches and why not see if you can get a video of your team playing to keep. It's always good fun looking back at old match clips on presentation night.

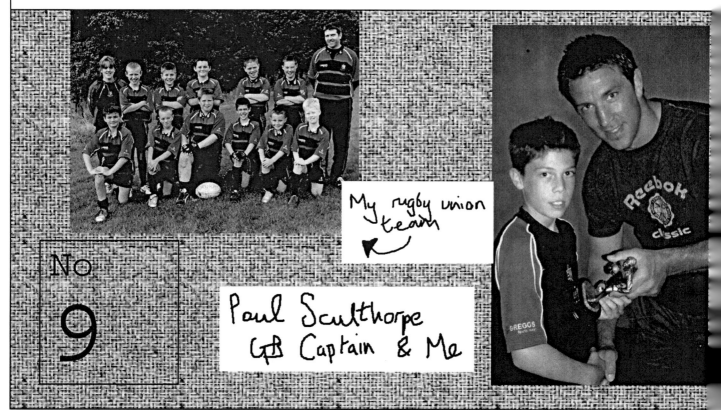

My rugby union team

No 9

Paul Sculthorpe
GB Captain & Me

Jonny's day at Twickenham

I will never forget the day I represented Sale Sharks in the 02 Kick, Pass and Run competition.

I had to compete against players from all the other Premiership clubs on the Twickenham pitch. I tried my best and I won. I couldn't believe I was the National Rugby Champion!!!!

Jason Leonard presented me with my trophy. One day I want to be like him and win the World Cup for England.

CJ's First Match

 I couldn't sleep I was so excited! I woke my dad up really early and we practiced.

I wasn't nervous about playing, I just wanted to have a good match.

My top tip is don't let anyone tell you that you can't play rugby.

I trained for six months before my first match and it was so worth it.

THE COACH DOCTOR

I'M HERE TO ANSWER ALL YOUR QUESTIONS

Hi Coachdoctor,
I really want to play rugby but I wear glasses.
I can't play because my glasses might fall off
and break. Is there anything I can do?
Love
Billy, aged ten, New Zealand.

Dear Billy,
I've got some great news for you. There are some
special goggles that you can get from your
opticians. They will let you see and they won't
fall off your head as you play because they have
an elastic strap on the back.
Coachdoctor

Hi Coachdoctor,
How can I find out the rugby rules?
Love from
Jamie, aged eleven, England.

Dear Jamie,
Every country has a rugby website (e.g. type in
England rugby) that has all the rules on so have
a look there. You could also ask your coach for
a copy.
Coachdoctor

14

Hi Coachdoctor,
I like watching rugby and I'd like to start playing but I'm scared I'm going to hurt myself tackling.
Love
Emma, aged 9, Ireland.

Dear Emma,
Lots of people are scared of tackling but please don't be worried. If you join a rugby team you will be coached by someone who can teach you how to tackle safely. You will have lots of practice before you play a game. You could be a great player so just give it a go.
Coachdoctor

Hi Coachdoctor,
I want to play rugby and join a team. What equipment do I need?
From
Luke, aged 6, Australia.

Dear Luke,
When you turn up for your first training session it's a good idea to wear a gum shield. A gum shield is a piece of plastic that fits in your mouth to protect your teeth. You can buy one very cheaply from your local sports shop. If you have rugby boots or football boots you can wear them to your first training session. Don't go out and buy boots though because you should wait a few weeks until you're sure you want to play rugby. Don't worry about buying a rugby kit just yet.
Coachdoctor

Chapter 2:

Rugby....Giving it your all

If you want to be the best at rugby you are going to have to change your lifestyle and approach. This means changing the way you do things. You have to become committed to getting better. You have to constantly try to get better, you can't simply be content with your current performance.

Before we begin please fill out the self evaluation form which measures how good you are at certain aspects of rugby. You should hope to score at least five in most of the categories. By the end of the book you should be able to boost up your scores quite a bit.

Top tip: It is impossible to score a 10 as everyone has room for improvement.

SELF EVALUATION FORM
AM I READY TO BE THE BEST?

I AM GOING TO FILL THIS FORM OUT AND THEN DO IT AGAIN IN SIX MONTHS TO SEE HOW MUCH I'VE IMPROVED.

I AM GOING TO BE HONEST WITH MYSELF BECAUSE THERE IS NO POINT IN CHEATING. I AM MARKING MYSELF OUT OF 10. 1 BEING POOR, 5 BEING AVERAGE AND TEN BEING OUTSTANDING.

BASIC SKILLS (PASSING AND CATCHING)	1	2	3	4	5	6	7	8	9	10
FITNESS	1	2	3	4	5	6	7	8	9	10
SPORTSMAN-SHIP	1	2	3	4	5	6	7	8	9	10
WILLINGNESS TO LEARN	1	2	3	4	5	6	7	8	9	10
DETERMINATION	1	2	3	4	5	6	7	8	9	10
LOVE OF THE GAME	1	2	3	4	5	6	7	8	9	10
KNOWLEDGE OF THE RULES	1	2	3	4	5	6	7	8	9	10
RESPECT FOR MY COACHES	1	2	3	4	5	6	7	8	9	10
SELF BELIEF	1	2	3	4	5	6	7	8	9	10
KICKING ABILITY	1	2	3	4	5	6	7	8	9	10
GAME EXPERIENCE	1	2	3	4	5	6	7	8	9	10
TRAINING SESSION ATTENDANCE	1	2	3	4	5	6	7	8	9	10

Respect

One of the pointers on the self evaluation sheet asked you to mark down how much you respect your coaches. This is the first thing we are going to discuss because your attitude to your coaches has a huge impact on how far you will go in the rugby world.

At the end of the day coaches want you to do well. The coaches you will have as a young player are unpaid volunteers who are kindly offering their services for free. It is important you respect your coaches or you could find yourself removed from a team or causing huge rifts in your team which damages teamwork.

"Coaches like to see selfless players, great players make others look good. If you do better than the challenge set then coaches will select you."

Graham Smith
International
Coach.

Respecting your coach

Remember coaches are human beings too so treat them with respect. If you give them respect, they'll give you respect back. You can always ask your coach questions about how you can improve. He or she will give you a few pointers. You need to accept what your weaknesses and strengths are.

Occasionally you might be coached by a person you don't like or have no respect for. You can change teams if that would make you feel better. Sometimes you can't because the coach is a regional coach and in this situation you might have to just grit your teeth and bare it. After a season you usually move up an age grade and your coach will change.

Getting advice from professional coaches

As well as asking your own coach for tips, you can learn from other coaches too. When you are watching an international match on TV don't turn off the TV as soon as the match finishes. Listen to what the two coaches, the commentators and the man of the match say at the end. They will give a report of what worked and what didn't. You can learn a lot. Try and read rugby magazines and rugby articles when you get chance.

Top coaching advice from Graham Smith

Graham Smith is a very experienced coach. He has coached the England Women's Forwards, played for England U23s and was an international prop for Scotland. He has ten top tips for young players.

Graham Smith's top ten tips:

1. If you want to improve your training/match day performance you need personal discipline and personal skill practice.

2. Concentrate hard on every task.

3. The best teams are those who have a collectively high work ethic and put in a lot of hard work.

4. It takes hard work to be the best. Get up faster than you get knocked down.

5. Be honest with yourself and the others you work closest with.

6. Don't cut corners.

7. You have to believe that your opponent is training harder than you.

8. Train like you are always no 2.

9. The best players in the world practice more than anyone else.

10. Know your position, know the position next to you, know your enemy.

MY PERSONAL STATEMENT

This book is crammed full of top tips from coaches and players. There are so many tips that it is easy to forget many of them as you continue reading. It's a good idea to use a highlighter pen or felt tip to underline important tips so you can easily find them later on.

It is also a good idea to write yourself a personal statement. In a personal statement you can list all the things you are going to do. You can include some of the tips you read about in this book. Your personal statement is private and can be used to inspire you to keep reaching for the top. You could make a copy of your personal statement and put it on the back of your bedroom door so you can see it every time you leave your room.

You can decorate your personal statement with glitter, drawings, photographs, magazine cuttings......it's up to you. Try and make it as eye catching as possible. There are a few points on your personal statement already but get going.....try and add another couple before moving on to the next page. Make sure you come back again and add something new after every chapter.

I AM GOING TO BE HONEST WITH MYSELF AND OTHERS.

I AM NOT GOING TO CHEAT AT TRAINING.

I AM ALWAYS GOING TO TRY MY VERY BEST.

STICK PICTURE OF
MYSELF HERE

SIGNED BY.................................

DATE...

<u>Top tips and wise words from England Rugby Union Women's team</u>

Before we move on have a look at what England Women's team have to say. Put a circle around the quotes you like the best. Think about how you can improve your game as you read.

"The biggest challenge I had to overcome was having to lose three stone when I started playing. If you want to be a great rugby player you have to not let anything stop you. If you get injured try not to let it knock your confidence."
Katy Storie, England Prop.

"Always make sure you have been eating well and hydrating especially leading up to a match. If your body doesn't have enough energy from the food you've eaten, it will struggle to work at the highest level during a game. This is also true of hydration- make sure you drink little and often."
Tamara Taylor, England Second Rower.

"When you are training and playing, you need to possess that extra bit of will power that says "I CAN keep going."
Tamara Taylor, England Second Rower.

"Last year I had the honour of playing in the World Cup in Canada. I was selected to play in all of the games, but was on the bench for the final. I was absolutely devastated. I had to overcome my disappointment and concentrate on doing the best I could, with what I had at the time."
Tamara Taylor, England Second Rower.

"Work hard on your set-piece as this is the bread and butter of a forward, but don't get bogged down with it, rugby is played by 15 players in open play."
Tamara Taylor, England Second Rower.

"As a centre you are part of the midfield unit and communication is key. It is key for a solid defensive wall and vital to producing innovative and inspiring attacking play."
Georgina Roberts, England Academy Centre.

"Use lots of self talk and imagery to prepare yourself for big games.
Strive to be the best player you can be. Many county players fall by the wayside because they lack that inner drive…you either want it or you don't."
Georgia Stevens, England Back Rower.

"Always ask coaches for feedback so you know what you need to improve on.
Then go away and work on it. Or ask them how to work on it. What you think you need to improve on might not be what you actually need to work on."
Leah Carey, England Backrower.

"Having what was expected of me being the same as all the ladies who had been elite for years was difficult at the start. Now I see it as an honour. "
Michaela Staniford, London Wasps Centre.

"As a young player the biggest challenge I had was learning rugby for the first time in a foreign language. I'm so glad I stuck with it…I got to lift the Grand Slam Trophy this year as England Captain!"
Sue Day, England Winger/Centre.

"To prepare for big matches I taper my training towards the end of the week and rest the day before apart from maybe a team run. I eat the correct food and make sure get enough rest and sleep. The night before I set myself personal goals that I want achieve in the game. On the morning of the game I try to stay relaxed and I focus on how I want to perform. When getting changed and warming up I really try and get in the zone of game mentality."
Sarah Hunter, England Flanker.

"Music is a really good method of preparation just before the game - we get motivational videos when playing for the Student's, Academy, and the A's, which include players in the team doing impressive stuff in a previous match all set to really motivational music."
Sam Dale, England Students Hooker.

"Don't be satisfied with mediocrity - always strive to be better than the no 1 in the world at your position."
Emma Layland, England Hooker.

"I make use of every opportunity I'm given both on and off the pitch. I make the choice to front up when we're losing and get stuck in because I know that's the time I'll learn most about rugby and more importantly about myself. I try to find the positive in all situations and lead by example."
Georgina Roberts, England Academy Centre.

The four Cs

You have to be commited to training if you want to be the best

There are four qualities that every rugby player needs. These are the four Cs:

Character
Commitment
Confidence
Calmness

No rugby player can be the best they can be without mastering the four Cs. You need all four qualities to be the best. Before we explore each quality let's find out if you are lacking any of the four Cs. On the opposite page is a short questionnaire for you to fill in. Put a tick next to the statements if they describe things you do. After you've filled out the questionnaire you should know which of the four Cs you need to work on.

THE FOUR C'S QUESTIONNAIRE

DATE:

1. IN MATCHES I SOMETIMES GET FRUSTRATED AND ARGUE WITH THE REF.

2. I GET VERY WORKED UP BEFORE MATCHES AND SOMETIMES I FEEL SICK.

3. I ONLY TURN UP TO TRAINING WHEN I CAN BE BOTHERED.

4. SOMETIMES I REFUSE TO SHAKE THE OPPOSITIONS HANDS AT THE END OF THE MATCH.

5. I DON'T LIKE PLAYING IN TOUGH MATCHES BECAUSE I'M AFRAID I'M GOING TO LET MY TEAM DOWN.

6. I GET VERY NERVOUS BEFORE EXAMS IN SCHOOL.

7. I DON'T CARE WHETHER I DO WELL IN SCHOOL OR NOT.

8. I DON'T GO TO TRAINING WHEN IT'S RAINING.

9. I CHEAT DURING TRAINING EXERCISES.

10. I'VE NOT PLAYED RUGBY FOR VERY LONG SO I DON'T THINK I'M AS GOOD AS THE OTHER PLAYERS IN MY TEAM.

11. I ONLY PICK UP A RUGBY BALL AT RUGBY TRAINING, I DON'T PRACTICE AT HOME.

12. SOMETIMES I SAY NASTY THINGS ABOUT OTHER MEMBERS OF MY TEAM.

13. IF I DON'T GET MY WAY AT HOME, I KICK UP A FUSS UNTIL MY MUM GIVES IN.

Answers to questionnaire

Question 1:   If you ticked question 1 you might need to work on your character.

Question 2:   If you ticked question 2 you might need to work on your calmness.

Question 3:   If you ticked question 3 you might need to work on your commitment.

Question 4:   If you ticked question 4 you might need to work on your character.

Question 5:   If you ticked question 5 you might need to work on your confidence.

Question 6:   If you ticked question 6 you might need to work on your calmness.

Question 7:   If you ticked question 7 you might need to work on your character.

Question 8:   If you ticked question 8 you might need to work on your commitment.

Question 9:   If you ticked question 9 you might need to work on your character.

Question 10:   If you ticked question 10 you might need to work on your confidence.

Question 11:   If you ticked question 11 you might need to work on your commitment.

Question 12:   If you ticked question 12 you might need to work on your character.

Question 13:   If you ticked question 13 you might need to work on your character.

FROM THE QUESTIONNAIRE I HAVE FOUND THAT I

NEED TO WORK ON ....

....

Character- the first C

To become a professional player you must have the right character. Some players don't and this stops them reaching their potential. Every player needs to learn what is acceptable and what isn't.

You need to have the right attitude at rugby training. If your coach wants you to jog twice around the pitch to warm-up then you need to do it. There's no point complaining and pretending to get a drink instead. This causes disruption and wastes time. If you start complaining then this spreads through the team.

Similarly if you are doing a handling exercise and one player keeps dropping the ball you mustn't make nasty comments or snigger. Everyone makes mistakes and every member of the squad needs encouragement.

Coaches pick up on players who have the wrong character. If you have the wrong character then this might make the coach think twice about selecting you for tournaments. Even the most talented player in the team might find himself on the subs bench if he doesn't show respect. All rugby players need respect for their team mates, coaches, match officials and parents.

This Canadian rugby union team is listening to their coach's advice while practicing lifting.

Commitment- the second C

You need to be committed to being the best.

You need to be fully focused. This means that you know where you want to be and you'll do everything that's needed to get there. It takes time to get better. You can't expect to go to bed one night and wake up in the morning a world class rugby player. You need to be committed to team training and training in your own time.

If you are fully committed to your team you shouldn't let bad weather or a bit of mud put you off. Professional players have to play whatever the weather so you should too.

If you are committed to improving your current performance you will read the whole of this book. If you are not committed you will only read half of it. Players who aren't committed soon get distracted and give up. They like the idea of being a better rugby player but they aren't willing to put the extra effort and training into becoming the best.

It takes real determination and commitment to win on muddy days.

Confidence- the third C

Confidence plays a key part in who wins rugby matches. If you think that a team cannot be beat then you will struggle to beat them. It is the same in any sport. Athletes sometimes feel that it is impossible to beat a world record but once someone beats it, lots of athletes beat the old record. This is because it is no longer seen as being impossible to beat.

How to build confidence.

THE TEN STEPS TO CONFIDENCE:

1. GET A PIECE OF PAPER AND SOME FELT TIPS.

2. TRY AND THINK ABOUT THE THINGS THAT MAKE YOU HAVE LESS CONFIDENCE.

3. WRITE THEM DOWN ON THE PIECE OF PAPER.

4. READ EACH THING ON YOUR LIST OUT LOUD.

5. USE A RED FELT TIP TO PUT A CROSS THROUGH EACH THING THAT MAKES YOU HAVE LESS CONFIDENCE.

6. NEXT TO WHERE YOU HAVE CROSSED OUT START WRITING A NEW LIST.

7. WRITE THE OPPOSITE OF WHAT YOU HAVE CROSSED OUT. WRITE IN CAPITAL LETTERS THIS TIME.

EXAMPLE:

I can never be as good as my brother.   I CAN BE AS GOOD AS MY BROTHER.

There are too many rules to learn.   I CAN LEARN THE RULES

8. READ EACH THING ON YOUR NEW LIST OUT LOUD.

9. ADD A PHOTOGRAPH OF YOURSELF PLAYING RUGBY.

10. STICK THE PAGE NEXT TO A MIRROR SO YOU CAN READ IT WHILE YOU'RE BRUSHING YOUR TEETH EVERY DAY.

Self belief can be more important than physical strength. You need to learn to believe in your ability. Follow the ten steps to confidence to get rid of the thoughts that are holding you back. Fill in the confidence box below.

I CAN BE THE BEST

LIST OF THINGS THAT ARE HOLDING ME BACK:

1. ....

....

....

2. ....

....

....

3. ....

....

....

4. ....

LIST OF CONFIDENT STATEMENTS:

1. ....

....

....

2. ....

....

....

3. ....

....

....

4. ....

MY PHOTO

Bullies

As you move up the rugby ranks you will meet people who say nasty things about other people. Some may even say nasty things about you. Bullies try to ruin people's confidence. You have to be strong and ignore them. You are a great player and they are only trying to put you down. Players who bully other players are usually feeling threatened because they aren't as good a player as the person they are bullying. Bullies are quitters, when things aren't going their way they head for the hills.

Never listen to anyone who says you're not going to make it.

"Never give up and have faith in yourself even when others put you down. I was once told I would never make a professional rugby player back in 1993. Three months later not only was I a professional rugby player I had also gained my first international senior cap."
Jason Critchley, former Welsh International.

Don't be a bully

Sometimes we can say something about a player in our team to make people laugh. If someone drops the ball we might make a joke about it. We might think that it's just a bit of fun but to some people it's not fun at all. The person you are joking about might feel very hurt and let down. You should always think about the other person's feelings. How would you feel if someone was laughing at you?

Rugby & Diabetes
Struan's story

I was diagnosed as a diabetic when I was thirteen. I loved rugby and I didn't want to give it up. I knew my team mate Jon had diabetes so I asked him about it. He said I could carry on playing as long as I monitored my blood sugar levels regularly, and did extra tests around games and training sessions. I was so glad I could keep on playing.

I always eat regular meals with enough carbohydrates, and I always ensure I have plenty of food and glucose drinks with me when I am exercising. I also look out for hypo's in the afternoon after a mornings rugby.

Spot the difference

It's easy to trick the opposition into thinking you are more confident than you really are. Your body language says a lot about you. Your body language is the way you stand or move about. Look at the two pictures below. Which player are you most like on match days?

Player 1

Player 2

Player 1's body language is the complete opposite of player 2's. Player 1 looks nervous and is staring at the floor. His hands are in his pockets. If you have your hands in your pockets you are telling the opposition that you are not ready to play, and that you don't want a pass. Player 1 is wearing tracksuit bottoms which show that he is a new player and doesn't like the cold. Tracksuit bottoms slow you up and within a couple of minutes they will be wet from the mud. It is much better to wear shorts. Player 1 also has muddy boots on before the game has even started. You should always clean your boots because dried on mud slows you down.

Player 2's body language makes him look confident. He stands up straight, with his head held high. He is wearing all the right kit. He looks calm and focused. He is staring straight ahead at the opposition.

Player 2 seems the most confident. Any opposition would see Player 1 as an easy target so would constantly attack in his direction. They would avoid Player 2 and kick in Player 1's direction. If you are new to a team, don't let the opposition know it. Stand like player 2 and pretend that you are the most confident person on the pitch. Check where you should stand before you get on the pitch, never ask once you're on the pitch because this shows that you are new. Do some stretches while you wait for the game to start. Prepare your mind and body for the match.

Calmness- the fourth c

Relaxing your body and mind before and after a game can drastically improve your performance. It is an area that most young players neglect. Relaxation can help you prepare for a big match and with practice it can help you learn to relax different muscles.

Relaxation also helps reduce stress so can be used to help not only your rugby but also at exam time at school.

To relax successfully it is important that you are in the right environment. You can't attempt relaxation in a room with a television blaring and people coming in and out. You need to find a quiet room where you can have time on your own without interruptions. The room needs to be dimly lit and warm.

Top tip: When stressed at school scrunch your fist up as tightly as possible. Hold it like this for ten seconds then release. You'll find yourself instantly becoming more relaxed.

Instead of reading how important relaxation is I want you to now try relaxation yourself. It's time to get physical. Follow the ten steps of relaxation and you'll be feeling a whole lot calmer. Go on, give it a go.

THE TEN STEPS TO RELAXATION

1. LIE DOWN ON YOUR BACK. GET IN A COMFORTABLE POSITION.

2. CLOSE YOUR EYES.

3. BEGINNING AT YOUR FEET AND WORKING YOUR WAY UPWARDS TO YOUR HEAD CONCENTRATE ON RELAXING EVERY MUSCLE IN TURN.

4. BREATHE THROUGH YOUR NOSE AND LISTEN TO YOURSELF BREATHING.

5. CONCENTRATE ON YOUR BREATHING AND FORGET EVERYTHING ELSE.

6. AS YOU BREATHE OUT SAY "ONE" TO YOURSELF. DON'T SAY IT OUT LOUD BUT SAY IT SILENTLY IN YOUR HEAD.

7. CONTINUE BREATHING AND REPEATING "ONE" EVERY TIME YOU BREATHE OUT.

8. KEEP DOING THIS FOR TEN MINUTES. YOU CAN CHECK THE TIME BUT YOU MUSTN'T SET AN ALARM.

9. ONCE YOUR TEN MINUTES ARE UP CARRY ON LYING QUIETLY. START WITH YOUR EYES CLOSED THEN OPEN THEM FOR A FEW MINUTES.

10. WHEN YOU ARE READY STAND UP AND LEAVE THE ROOM.

Now you know all about the four Cs its time you flipped back to your personal statement. Try and add some of the things we've talked about in the last chapter.

Now you have read all about the four Cs it's time to test yourself by completing the big four Cs word search challenge. All the words in the word search are from this chapter.

THE BIG FOUR CS WORD SEARCH CHALLENGE

C	C	S	S	E	N	M	L	A	C	R
C	O	M	M	I	T	M	E	N	T	R
O	R	R	M	R	U	G	B	Y	B	R
N	M	T	S	E	B	D	N	S	R	E
F	A	A	D	N	A	T	S	T	E	T
I	E	L	R	E	L	A	X	N	A	C
D	T	B	U	L	L	Y	O	I	T	A
E	S	P	I	T	S	E	N	O	H	R
N	L	A	N	O	S	R	E	P	I	A
C	H	E	A	T	O	W	E	N	N	H
E	D	E	S	S	E	R	T	S	G	C
O	D	T	N	E	M	E	T	A	T	S

CONFIDENCE	TEAM	BULLY
CALMNESS	CHEAT	TIPS
COMMITMENT	CHARACTER	DO
BEST	RELAX	NEW
BREATHING	HONEST	STAND
PERSONAL	POINTS	RUGBY
STATEMENT	STRESSED	

THE COACH DOCTOR

I'M HERE TO
ANSWER ALL YOUR
QUESTIONS

Hi Coachdoctor,
I'm going my first training session on Wednesday.
I'm a bit nervous. I used to play for another
team but I was bullied so I quit. I haven't
played for a year. I'm scared my new team will
bully me.
Love
Aaron, aged nine, Germany.

Dear Aaron,
I'm so sorry that you got bullied in your old
team. It's great news that you're starting
playing again. Please don't be nervous about
going your first training session with your new
team. I'm sure your new team won't bully you.
They'll be thrilled to have you play for them.
You'll be a great part of their team. Just go
along and have fun.
Coachdoctor

Hi Coachdoctor,
I read what you said about being confident but I have a bit of a problem. I love playing rugby and I'm quite good at it. I have long hair and sometimes during matches other players accidentally pull my hair. They don't mean to but it hurts so much. What can I do?
Love
Chloe, aged eight, France.

Dear Chloe,
You are not alone! Lots of players have the same problem. It's a good idea to tie your hair back. The best idea is to ask someone to braid it. This makes sure it is kept out of the way. Another idea is to wear a skull cap. A skull cap is a hat that rugby players wear. It is usually worn to protect a player's head in scrums but it will also keep your hair out of the way too.
Coachdoctor

Hi Coachdoctor,
I've got a big match on Sunday and I'd love to have someone there to watch me play. My mum has got to work. Should I ask my granddad?
From
David, aged five, Wales.

Dear David,
Yes!!!!
Ask your granddad. I'm sure he'd love to come and watch you play. Quite a few players have their granddads at matches.
Coachdoctor

Chapter 3:

Rugby.... Your fitness

In this chapter you will improve your fitness level. Every sportsman or woman needs to be fit and this is even more important in rugby. In a rugby match you are on the go all the time and you cover quite a lot of distance in the time between the first whistle and the last.

Some players have the raw ability to be great rugby players but their fitness level lets them down and they can only play to a high level for a few minutes. Professional players and those in regional teams have to be able to play for the full match and still have enough energy to carry on if there is extra time to be played.

If you detest doing extra training then you need to get used to it if you want to climb higher up the rugby ladder. Professional players are paid to train for several hours every day. Great kickers like Johnny Wilkinson are only great because they practice every day. Johnny even practices his kicking on Christmas Day. He is committed to being the best player he can be.

Physical fitness

It is a good idea to schedule your time in a fitness planner. Make sure you always give yourself one full day off a week. You might join a cricket team, go swimming or go for a jog. You need to be realistic in what you commit yourself to do. There's no point promising to do loads if you're going to stop after a week. If you struggle committing large amounts of time to extra practice maybe build up gradually over a few weeks. Set yourself a little reward after you've completed a few weeks to encourage yourself to keep going. You might treat yourself to a new pair of trainers or a weekend off. It will be hard to keep going initially but after a while it becomes part of your routine.

"If you don't use it you'll lose it!"
Don't think that if you spend a couple of weeks doing your fitness planner then stop that you'll still be fitter than when you started. Training effects are reversible. The benefit the exercise has given you will disappear if you reduce your exercise time or stop completely. It's very important that you keep going with your exercise routine. If you miss one week's training it can take up to three weeks of training to get you back to the same level. The important thing is to keep going.

Small changes

There are many little things you can do that will make a big difference to your fitness level. You can try to walk more. If you can, why not walk to and from school every day? You could cycle to rugby training instead of making your parents drive you. If you mess around with a rugby ball every day you will soon see that your handling skills improve. Doing a few sit-ups and press-ups every day will help too.

Finding a training buddy

Why not ask one of your rugby mates to train with you. It's harder to cancel a training session if you're going to be letting someone down. It also helps someone else get fitter too. Maybe your mum or brother would go jogging with you once a week, you don't know until you ask.

Kicking practice is so much easier when you are with a buddy. Instead of kicking all the balls over the posts and then having to collect them, your buddy can kick them back to you. It saves you time and allows you more opportunities to kick. Your buddy can also put you under pressure when you are about to kick, which helps you get into the match day frame of mind.

Please turn your book onto its side so you can read properly.

Making a fitness planner

Now is the time to commit yourself to training. Have a look at the example and then make your own fitness planner. Starting today, you are going to work harder on your fitness levels.

40

FITNESS PLANNER

EXAMPLE:

TUES	WEDS	THURS	FRI	SAT	SUN
SCHOOL TEAM TRAINING (1 HOUR)	PE AT SCHOOL (1 HOUR)	SCHOOL TEAM MATCH	TENNIS (1 HOUR)	SWIMMING (1 HOUR)	RUGBY MATCH
KICKING PRACTICE (30 MINS)	CLUB TRAINING (1 HOUR)	KICKING PRACTICE (30 MINS)	PRACTICE MY PASSING (15 MINS)	PRACTICING MY PASSING (15 MINS)	

NOTES:

MONDAY IS MY DAY OFF....REST.
ON THURSDAY KICKING PRACTICE GO WITH BEN. START AT 7PM.

MY FITNESS PLANNER

DATE STARTED:

MON	TUES	WEDS	THURS	FRI	SAT	SUN

NOTES:

As part of your training schedule you can play other sports. This will add variety and can be loads of fun. Many of the top rugby players combine their rugby training with football, cricket, tennis, golf, swimming or boxing.

Football can help you develop your pace and work on your footwork.

Cricket can help your ball control as you adjust to throwing and catching a smaller ball.

Boxing is a good way to learn how to channel your anger.

Tennis is a good way of building up your arms after an injury.

Another benefit of playing other sports is that you get to play in other teams. You can see how other teams operate. When you become a professional player you will play for a few teams so it's good to see how easily you fit into other teams.

<u>My rugby story</u>
<u>Kevin George, Wales U18 coach</u>

The skills that you gain from other sports can be transferred to rugby. For instance if you have always been a footballer but you've recently took up rugby, don't worry. The skills you got from football can help you on the rugby pitch. Give yourself time to adjust. Enjoy it and play for fun. What will come your way will come your way.

Making it as a professional rugby player depends on your mental approach. Most fail when they join an academy or big club . You need to be mentally strong. Many experience big fish syndrome : they're used to being the big stars and then they have to start at the beginning again. Self discipline is key. Physicality is important as is being part of something.

It is dangerous to train too much as it adds pressure to your body. You need to train in moderation and give yourself a full day off each week. Listen to your own body. If you feel exhausted give yourself a few days off to recover. You don't need to train every second of the day. Go out with your mates to the cinema or play on the playstation....spend time relaxing and enjoying other things.

Never let your fitness schedule get in the way of your school work. You can't afford to neglect your school life because every rugby player needs something to fall back on. Rugby careers are relatively short and you will need to get a job when you finish.

If you get ill you must stop training until you are fully better. You need to let your body rest and mend itself.

My rugby story

My name's Daniel Musto and I play for Bradford and Bingley. Rest is important and you need to take care of your body. You should never be afraid to take some time out to let your body recover.

Last season I was captain of Bradford and Bingley colts (this is like the academy. You have to be under eighteen to play), I also played for the first team and played for Yorkshire. This put a lot of strain on my body and left me feeling a bit drained.

The colts had an important semi-final coming up, versus the team who won the previous season. We really wanted to win the West Yorkshire Cup so I had an important decision to make. I took it upon myself to withdraw from the senior side for a week, to help my body rest. This could have had many negative effects:

1. The replacement player taking my place in the first team.
2. Getting injured because I wasn't used to prolonged periods of rest.
3. Both the colts and the first team losing, wasting all my efforts.

In the end, it was all worth it. We beat the previous year's winners and progressed to the final. I really believe resting my body was key and vital to our success.

Diet

Diet is important for all sports people. Your body needs food so that it can work properly. You need to eat breakfast so that you can give 100% at rugby training. It is important that you eat lots of fruit and vegetables. If you don't eat right your performances will suffer.

You can eat burgers, chips and chocolate but really you should only eat them as a treat. You need to look after your body. Don't worry if you find reducing the fast food you eat hard. Even professional players struggle. Rodney So'oialo who plays for New Zealand admits that he doesn't have much self control when it comes to food. He loves KFC.

Water is really important and you should always make sure you drink plenty of it during a training session. During matches when the waterboy runs on make sure you have a sip or two, it really helps.

As you grow older some of your friends will start drinking, smoking and taking drugs. If you really want to be the best you should stay clear of all three. Some professional players cheat and take drugs to make them play better. This is a big mistake and they let so many people down. Drinking and smoking will prevent you reaching the top of your potential. The best players in the world want to succeed so much that they won't pollute their bodies with alcohol, cigarettes or drugs.

My rugby story

Last season the team I support won a big final which meant they were going up into the highest league. Everyone in my town was so excited and we all went down to the club to see the trophy and congratulate the players. I was looking forward to meeting my favourite player and getting his autograph.

When I saw my favourite player I was shocked. He had a cigarette in one hand and a beer bottle in the other. He was signing authograph's for people but kept spilling the beer as he wrote. In the end he gave the beer bottle to some kids to hold and said they could have a sip if they wanted.

I was so shocked. None of the other player were drunk like him. I couldn't believe he was letting kids drink. I decided he wasn't my favourite player any more.

This season he wasn't playing for my team. My Dad said it was because he was an okay player but he wasn't good enough for the highest league. Maybe if he didn't get drunk or smoke he'd be a better player. He wasn't a good role model for anyone.

Sarah Sparks, aged 11

FITNESS AND DIET TIPS

"Train like mad in the summer. Don't lose sight of the season ahead. You can gain so much in the summer holidays. I improved my kicking and passing game loads during this time."
Tom Dugarin, King's College School.

"Ask your coaches and see what you need to develop. You can work on these things before and after training even if it's just 10 minutes or do some extras in your back garden. If you get used to doing that when you're younger it's a trait you'll have for life and you don't have to learn to do it when you're older."
Jason Golden, Wakefield Wildcats.

"There is always room for improvement on your cardio, so if you have ten minutes to spare or an hour, go running."
Spencer, Lester B. Pearson High School.

"Always make sure you have been eating well and hydrating especially leading up to a match. If your body doesn't have enough energy from the food you've eaten, it will struggle to work at the highest level during a game. This is also true of hydration- make sure you drink little and often."
Tamara Taylor, England International Second Rower.

"Rugby is probably the best example of "you get out what you put in." The harder you train the better you become!"
Rick Barrow, England.

"The best advice I can give from a players perspective is that to be successful on the field, you have to work your butt off when your off the field, training is the key to success, especially in the fast paced world of rugby."
Nick Betts, America.

"You can achieve your goals. I wanted to play in the RFU County Championship for NLD but I hadn't played rugby for three years. I wanted it so badly that I trained four times a week for two years...and this summer I achieved my goal. If you want it, go for it."
Rick Barrow, England.

"If you want to be the best and become a professional player one day you need to embrace extra practice and not avoid difficult activities and fitness training."
Josh Stump, Canada.

"You need to be committed and have heart. Come to 7am morning practices no matter what the circumstance... Our rugby team barely missed a practice. None of us knew how to play rugby when practice started, but then a month later, we made it to the playoffs. We were the underdogs in Tier 2. No matter what your size is, you can take anybody down."
Mahdin Al-Benghalee, America.

"No excuses. If you finish a game blowing really hard, then you haven't put the fitness work in at training. When you are training, train. Don't chat about the weekend etc. If you push yourself as hard as you can at every training session the games will become much easier."
Adam Clarke, Earlsdon RFC.

"Attend practice, always believe you can get better and believe the others around you can make you better. Do not get angry at a teammate who tries to correct you, even if he's wrong listen to the criticism and decide whether to use it or discard it."
Jeffrey Fell, USA International U17s.

"Conditioning is so important. It's a guarantee that you'll do your best sprinting down the field to score that try."
Vladimir L, Canada.

"If you want to become the best in your position you need to practice with an older player who already plays in your position. You can learn things from him by demonstration or by watching."
Chris Barry, Trojans RFC.

Mental preparation

Lots of players make the mistake of thinking that preparing themselves physically is enough to make them the best. They train hard before big matches, go every training session but fail to prepare their minds. Your mind is so important on match days. Top coaches realise that they have to make sure their players have good mental skills.

We are now going to look at the areas of fitness that are not used by many average rugby players. If you develop these skills you will improve your match day performance.

Mental toughness

All players need mental toughness. They need to be able to focus their minds on doing something successfully, even when placed under immense pressure. In World Cup's players have to kick penalties with thousands of people watching them in the stadium, and millions of people watching at home. They know that if they miss their team might be knocked out. Kicking a goal in those situations is completely different from practicing kicking on an empty pitch back home. Players are only able to successfully kick goals in big matches because they have prepared themselves mentally. When they go for the kick they are focusing on the kick and nothing else, so don't feel thousands of eyes watching them.

Mental toughness can be taught. You can improve your mental skills through match experience, trial and error and by trying different techniques.

Mental preparation for competitions

To prepare yourself for competitions and big matches you need to stimulate competition situations. That means practicing as if it was the real thing. Often competition games are a lot shorter than normal matches so you don't have all the time in the world to take a kick. You need to practice kicking in the time you will have in the competition.

If you are playing a friendly match a few weeks before a competition then during the match you need to pretend it's the final of the competition. You need to give it everything. If you tell yourself that losing the friendly is the same as losing the competition you will get yourself used to being under pressure.

If you simulate competition situations in you training schedule you will have a lot more confidence during competition games. Your mind will know that you have successfully completed similar tasks in the past so you will be more likely to kick that goal or score that try.

Ego and task motivation

There are two main types of motivation. There is ego orientation which means you are playing rugby because you want to be the winner and there is task orientation which means you are playing rugby because you enjoy being the best by improving your personal best performances.

What type of motivation do you have?

I HAVE ....TYPE OF MOTIVATION.

Don't worry if you think you have both types of motivation. You can have both. It's better to have high ego and high task orientation or be high in task orientation and low in task orientation. If you have this type of motivation you are a hard working person and do not give up when things are not working out.

The type of motivation you don't want is to be high in ego orientation and low in task orientation. People who have this type of motivation give up when they start to lose games.

Self talk

Many players across the world use self talk to help them be the best. Self talk simply means talking to yourself inside your head, while you are playing a match. You might say "tackle hard, tackle hard," "go, go, go" or "I can do this." If you say to yourself "I am going to win," you are more likely to win. It makes you try harder.

Self talk can also help you when you are kicking a penalty. Even if the crowd is shouting you can focus your mind. You might be nervous about missing the goal but if you say to yourself "I've kicked from this angle a hundred times and scored so I can do it now," you'll kick a lot more confidently.

Setting goals

Setting goals and targets can improve your match confidence greatly. It can also increase your motivation to succeed and improve the quality of your training. If you set yourself goals and then achieve them, you get a real sense of achievement and pride.

Now it's time to get working again and think up some realistic goals. You need small goals at first, there's no point setting yourself a big goal that you can't achieve. Make sure you reward yourself if you achieve a goal and if you find a goal is a bit too tough to tackle at once try breaking it down into smaller goals. Never feel guilty of failure.

MY GOALS

FOR THE NEXT MONTH:

WHEN I ACHIEVE THESE GOALS I WILL TREAT MYSELF TO:

FOR THE REST OF THE SEASON:

WHEN I ACHIEVE THESE GOALS I WILL TREAT MYSELF TO:

FOR NEXT SEASON:

WHEN I ACHIEVE THESE GOALS I WILL TREAT MYSELF TO:

"Set yourself small reachable goals, as this will progress your performance over a period of time. Chasing a massive goal will often leave players failing or giving in, whereas, many realistic and smaller goals will allow you to see change over time."

Daniel Musto, Bradford and Bingley, and Yorkshire

Imagery and visualisation is a good way of preparing yourself mentally for rugby. Imagery and visualisation simply means imagining that you are doing something. In a way it is day dreaming about lifting a trophy or scoring a try. You are imaging what it will be like. Preparing yourself mentally can help your decision making skills. It can help you pass better and score more tries.

"Think how it would feel to be the best, imagine yourself at the big grounds, singing the anthem and scoring that try. That should be enough motivation if someone really wanted it."
Michaela Staniford, England International Centre.

Johnny Wilkinson has said that he believes the psychology of kicking is very important. When he's taking a kick he visualises the ball travelling along its path and imagines how the ball will feel when it hits his foot. This helps him kick the ball accurately.

The warm up

It is just as important to warm up your mind before a match as it is to warm up your body. You might try watching some sport on TV the morning before a match to get you in the competitive frame of mind. When you are doing your stretches in the changing room before a match try and use imagery and visualisation to get your mind working. For instance, if you are a prop imagine the first scrum. Think about where you will put your feet, going down, the ball going in...

We warm up for three reasons: to improve our performance, to prevent injury and to prepare mentally for the event.

Always remember to cool down after a match. You need to stretch out and get out of the competitive frame of mind. Cooling down reduces stiffness.

Visual awareness

When England won the World Cup they had a visual awareness coach called Sherylle Calder. Visual awareness is about using your eyes and training them to be better. It is important that you have good vision skills. This doesn't mean that people who wear glasses aren't good players. It just means improving your eyes to keep you alert and to help your decision making. In modern matches everything happens so fast, on and off the ball, that you need to have an all around awareness of what's going on.

Communication is so important. You need to learn how to read the game and communicate with your team mates. There's no point seeing a gap in the defensive wall if you can't communicate to other players in your team. You need to tell the other players where the gap is.

Sherylle Calder believes that the biggest opportunities in defence and attack come from players simply seeing the space on the rugby pitch. Her job is to train players to use their eyes better. She says that the eye is a muscle and can be trained , exercised and measured in its performance.

The simplest way you can improve your visual awareness is by looking up and taking in all the pitch while you are playing. Most players only look up when they have the ball because they are constantly watching where the ball is. If you play like this, by the time you get the ball you have to waste valuable time looking for a gap. If you had already looked around you would know where the gaps are and also where the other players are for support. This improves your reaction time and gives you the edge. It will be hard to get into the habit of looking around but in time it will come naturally.

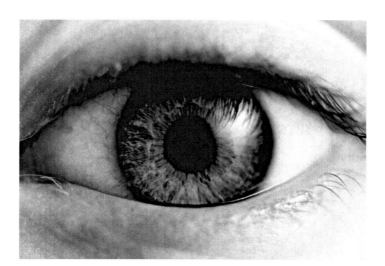

Improving your visual skills

You don't need a visual awareness coach to improve your visual skills. Try and complete all the challenges below. Put a tick next to a challenge once you have done it. Aim to do each challenge at least four times.

THE EYE SPY CHALLENGE

1. PRACTICE PASSING WITH DIFFERENT OBJECTS. TRY AND PICK OBJECTS THAT ARE A FUNNY SHAPE OR THAT ARE SMALLER THAN A RUGBY BALL.

   EXAMPLE: A TENNIS BALL, A PAIR OF SOCKS, A BANANA, A PING PONG BALL, A SHOE.

2. PRACTICE BOUNCING AND CATCHING A BOUNCY BALL. ONCE YOU'VE GOT THE HANG OF IT STOOD STILL, TRY DOING IT WHILE MOVING.

3. LEARN TO JUGGLE WITH TWO BALLS THEN TRY THREE.

4. PLAY EYE SPY WITH YOUR EYES CLOSED SO YOU CAN'T LOOK AROUND.

5. WHEN YOU'RE IN A CAR TRY TO READ ROAD SIGNS AND LICENCE PLATES OUT OF THE CORNER OF YOUR EYE, WITHOUT MOVING RIGHT OR LEFT.

THE COACH DOCTOR

I'M HERE TO ANSWER ALL YOUR QUESTIONS

Hi Coachdoctor,
Last week I hurt my leg at rugby training. I was tackling someone and they fell on my leg. I carried on playing but after the match it really hurt. I didn't tell my dad because he is really busy at work and I didn't want to worry him. I thought it would stop hurting after a while but it still hurts. Should I tell my dad now?
Love from
Samuel, aged eight, England.

Dear Samuel,
You need to tell your dad straight away. It is important that you tell someone when you hurt yourself. Your dad loves and cares for you so he wants you to tell him if you get hurt. He will know what to do next. It might be a good idea to go the doctors and get it checked out. It might be that you have to rest it for a while.
Coachdoctor

Hi Coachdoctor,
I want to practice my passing and catching skills
everyday but I can't because I have no one to
practice with. We live on a farm and none of my
team live near me. I don't have any brothers or
sisters and my parents are too busy working to
help me. Is there anything I can do?
Love from
Ben, aged nine, Canada.

Dear Ben,
I know it seems like you can't practice your
passing and catching but you can. You can bounce
your ball against a wall and then catch it. It's
a good idea to practice on a wall without any
windows…I'm sure your parents don't want any
smashed windows. You can also improve your
handling skills by weaving the ball around your
legs. As you do this more and more, you will get
better at it. You will be able to go faster and
faster…it will impress your team mates at
training.
Coachdoctor

Hi Coachdoctor,
I'm going to start jogging with my mum on
Tuesdays. We've both decided to get fitter.
Have you any top tips for us?
Love
Katie, aged twelve, Northern Ireland.

Dear Katie,
What a great idea! I'm sure you'll both benefit
loads from the extra exercise. The first tip
I'll give you is don't quit. If you can't run
anymore try walking for a bit and then start
running again. Your first jog will be tough but
it'll get easier every week. My second tip is
that you should wear some reflective vests or
bands if you are jogging in the autumn/winter
months. This makes sure that cars can see you
coming! Good luck.
Coachdoctor

Chapter 4:

Rugby.... The team

We've explored how you can work individually to be the best, now we're going to look at what makes a great team. Everyone remembers great teams of the past....one day you could be a player in a team that goes down in history as one of the best team ever.

Try and name two or three outstanding teams. They might be local teams, international teams or junior teams....it's completely up to you. If you get stuck why not ask your family who they think are the best rugby teams.

THE THREE TEAMS I THINK ARE OUTSTANDING:

1.

2.

3.

What type of team is my team?

There are two main types of rugby team. Put a tick next to the statements that best describe your team.

TEAM QUESTIONNAIRE

DATE:

1. MOST OF OUR TRIES ARE SCORED BY ONE PERSON.

2. OUR TRIES ARE SCORED BY LOTS OF PEOPLE.

3. WE MESS AROUND A LOT AT TRAINING.

4. WE DON'T ALWAYS WIN BUT WE HAVE LOTS OF FUN.

5. WE ALWAYS WELCOME NEW PLAYERS.

6. WE DON'T CARE IF WE INJURE SOME OF THE OPPOSITION.

7. WE LISTEN TO OUR COACHES.

8. WE ARGUE WITH OUR COACHES AND WITH EACH OTHER SOMETIMES.

9. WE DON'T BOTHER TURNING UP FOR TRAINING MOST OF THE TIME.

<u>Answers to questionnaire</u>

Question 1:	If you ticked question 1 you might belong to a selfish approach team.
Question 2:	If you ticked question 2 you might belong to a professional approach team.
Question 3:	If you ticked question 3 you might belong to a selfish approach team.
Question 4:	If you ticked question 4 you might belong to a professional approach team.
Question 5:	If you ticked question 5 you might belong to a professional approach team.
Question 6:	If you ticked question 6 you might belong to a selfish approach team.
Question 7:	If you ticked question 7 you might belong to a professional approach team.
Question 8:	If you ticked question 8 you might belong to a selfish approach team.
Question 9:	If you ticked question 9 you might belong to a selfish approach team.

Professional approach teams always give 100% and are made up of the best sort of rugby players. Selfish approach teams are made up of players who only care about themselves. They are not interested in the team.

FROM THE QUESTIONNAIRE I HAVE FOUND

THAT MY TEAM IS A ....

TYPE OF TEAM.

Winning and Losing

Every team has high and low points. You will win matches and you will lose matches. The best teams are the teams that can deal with the highs and lows and keep on going.

Everyone loves winning. The rush of adrenaline makes every bruise worth it. It's great to celebrate with your team mates and parents. Lifting the trophy and receiving your medal is amazing. Knowing that you've made a difference, whether it was scoring a try or making a big tackle, is a great confidence boost. There are always teams that you love beating, maybe they beat you last season and now you've scored thirty points against them.

Everyone hates losing. It doesn't matter if you win twenty matches then lose one...it still hurts. Everyone feels deflated and gutted. You start asking 'what if.' The important thing is that as a team you learn from your mistakes. Sometimes it's best to just forget about losing a match and move on. Train harder and be determined that you'll beat them next time. If that's not very realistic then maybe aim to reduce the points difference.

What to do when you lose

Don't be a bad loser!
Don't blame the ref!
Don't blame members of your team!

Shake hands with the opposition.
Don't cry however much it hurts.
Don't storm off!

"Be humble in victory and honest in defeat but at all times be proud to have been part of the game."
Crawley RFC Junior Girls.

"Success is something that should be realised and appreciated without being big headed. Failure is something that with strong mental attitude can be over come."
St Mary's Old Boys RFC U13s, Gloucestershire Champions.

Teamwork

There's no 'I' in the word team. Instead of being fifteen individuals you have to become one team. If you can, travel to tournaments together on a coach or minibus. Everyone needs to wear matching kit. So many teams have players in different socks, it looks horrible and stops them looking like one unit.

When you go and play as a team, walk around the rugby club and grounds together. Make sure that you're always seen as a group, never on your own. When you've got a gap between matches don't mess about. Go into the changing room or find some space away from everyone and practice.

Never warm up before matches with complicated passing exercises. Other teams will be watching you warm up and will see if you are constantly dropping the ball because the exercise is too complicated. NEVER play with a football at a rugby tournament. You are there to play rugby so focus your mind on the hard matches to come.

When its time to play a match let the other team line up first. Just before kick off walk onto the pitch as a team and line up. There's a lot of waiting around so there's no point getting on the pitch ten minutes early if it's cold.

At tournaments you might not play every match. In tight games coaches usually don't bring on the subs. Accept your coach's decision and don't pester to go on. Definitely don't argue because this will distract the players on the pitch. If you are subbed you can still be an asset to the team if you take responsibility for bringing on water bottles and the kicking cone. As soon as your team scores run on the pitch with the kicking cone so your kicker can get on with his job. In tournaments matches are sometimes only ten minutes

60

long so time is limited. So many teams lose matches because they waste valuable minutes searching for their kicking cone.

How parents can help

Encourage your child to go to bed early the night before a match. Matches are very tiring and your child will benefit from having the extra sleep.

You need to nominate one parent in the team to be in charge of the rules. Every tournament is different so you need someone who can concentrate on finding the rules in the match programme and note down the scores and points. This is important because when a final is tied sometimes the referee makes a mistake and goes against the tournament rules. For instance the referee might say there's going to be extra time when the tournament rules say the team that's scored the most tries should win. If your team has scored the most tries you need to appeal and claim the trophy. If you fail to appeal then you could lose the tournament.

Support your child whether they win or lose. There are always other games and tournaments.

Don't be the angry parent on the touchline. Stay calm. You can cheer for the team but don't go over the top. Don't shout at the referee or opposition coaches.

When you get home after a match make sure your child has a bath. It's important they relax their muscles.

Friendship

Having good friends at school and in your rugby team will help you be
the best. The best teams are made up from strong friends who stick
together no matter what. Good friends will help you when you're
feeling down. There are all sorts of people in rugby teams, people from
all kind of backgrounds and home lives. It doesn't matter how much
money you have or don't have, which school you go to or what your
parents are like. The one thing you share with the other players is a love
of rugby. Many adults today are still friends with people they played
rugby with when they were younger. You also get to know opposition
players after you've played against them season after season, and in
years to come you might end up at university with them. That's one of
the reasons why you should always shake hands after the match. You
don't want to be seen as a poor loser and when you play in adult
teams everyone goes back into the club for a drink.

Younger players have to learn that they can't just pass to their mates.
It's a bad habit and can alter the result of a game. You should be
willing to pass to everyone. Every team has a couple of players who
aren't very good at passing and catching but it's important that you
still pass to them. If you don't they'll never get better. They could even
drop out of the team because they never get a chance in a game.
Some players think this would be a good thing but it never is. You don't
know how much of an asset that player could be in the future. One
day you could be a man short and have to forfeit a big match
because you don't have enough, or this player with hands like a sieve
might develop into a 6ft giant who can score with ease. Everyone
develops at different speeds.

Hard times

Your friendships will be put to the test during your many seasons as a rugby player. Non-playing friends might complain because you don't go out with them much because you've got training or have to have an early night before a big match. Good friends will accept that you want to succeed at rugby and won't give you a hard time about it. Non-committed rugby players don't worry about missing training sessions, it's a bad habit to get into. Missing training sessions can actually be very dangerous. In the step up from playing tag rugby to playing full contact it is important that you attend every session. You need to learn how to tackle correctly and safely. It is also important in every other age group as you will fail to understand set moves and game plans if you continually miss training sessions.

If you are cocky and always imagine you will be your team's scrumhalf (or hooker, prop etc.) you are very wrong. It takes a lot of hard work to keep your position. You can't afford to miss training sessions because you will fall behind. Someone else could join your team who is a challenger to your position and if you aren't turning up to training your coach will pick him or her on match days. It isn't fair on your teammates if they go training every week and you don't. You are holding them back and restricting their success.

Changing position isn't always a bad thing. Your coach has the team's best interests at heart. Try not to treat your change of position as a let down. People change as they grow up. If you were scrumhalf for your team when you were nine it might be that you'd be better as hooker when you're thirteen. Don't punish the person who takes your old position, it's not their fault. Teach them what you can and never say nasty things about them to your team mates.

Building a great team

You should get to know your team mates off the field. This will help you become a better team. Why don't you go out as a team? You could go bowling or the cinema. Go and watch your favourite team play with a few of your team mates. After the match talk about who played well and what you can learn from watching your favourite stars play.

If a team mate keeps missing training because their Mum works during the evenings why not ask if you can give them a lift. You should encourage people at your school to come to rugby training. They might enjoy it and then you'll have some great new players!
After training why not go as a team into the club and play some pool and have a drink. It's great for building team spirit and it gives your parents a chance to chat. It also raises some money for your club.

How to be a top team

North Dorset RFC Girls U14

We finished last season undefeated and have only lost one match (friendly) this season. Ten girls play for Dorset County who are South West winners, seven play for the regional South West side and out of these two girls were picked for England's 'gifted and talented' squad. Several North Dorset RFC players recently won the Daily Telegraph National Emerging Schools final at Twickenham while playing for their school team, Gillingham.

Part of succeeding and becoming the best you can, starts with your own self belief.

Our training/match day tips

You need regular training sessions- looking at fitness, basic handling and match skills on a regular basis. It is essential to work on tackling techniques to give confidence and match winning abilities. Disciplined ruthlessness and commitment on the matchdays- it's all about playing not necessarily winning, but with the skills and discipline, should always be confident.

How we prepare for big matches

We prepare by having regular training and matches to hone the edges. Encouragement and explanation of the event, what comes next, what is the process and what the overall event means. For big matches and finals we try to have a calming influence, drawing upon training techniques and basic skills. We remember to play as a team and not individuals.

Coach's viewpoint....what special qualities do we have that makes us so successful?

We have honesty. It is essential to be honest- if mistakes have been made say so but give answers and put them right. Motivation is necessary to get that extra effort and to stay to the plan and basic skills. My team have really good individual and collective skills especially the ability to tackle ruthlessly, which certainly has snuffed out any real attack, and they always support each other in open play. They remain disciplined and keep their match playing tactical shape even under real pressure.

<u>What makes some players stand out from the rest and how can a player improve their chances of being selected?</u>

The players that stand out have running balance, fitness and speed, handling, tackling, awareness of other players and the opposition. You can improve your chances of being selected by continuing to learn the basics, being committed and always listening to advice and criticism. Be prepared to listen and learn from the most experienced.

<u>Dealing with success and failure</u>

Always put it into perspective. If hugely successful, try and find some real hard opposition to bring the sense of normality back and break the invincible attitude. If failing, encourage more commitment and training without putting anyone down- success does come with practice.

<u>Our greatest victory and our toughest match</u>

Our greatest victory was during the Emerging School semi finals at Stains on 5th May 2007. We had four matches to get through the pool to be in the final at Twickenham and we won all of them without conceding a single try. Balancing emotion and apprehension before the final was difficult but as soon as the whistle blew the girls played outstanding, supporting and committed to win. We didn't concede a single try and became National Champions.

Our toughest match last season was in the National 7s at Harpenden against a very strong Welsh Girls team who were both physical and strong. Although losing, the girls played well against a much stronger side and even with injuries, they still wanted to play on.

<u>Our tips for people joining a rugby team for the first time</u>

Go for it!!!!!!!!!

It sure beats sitting in front of the TV or computer screen. You can get fit, enjoy team sports where you rely on others and they rely on you. Rugby can cause injuries but so can any sport. Learn the basics first, have the right equipment and attitude, as this means injuries are less likely to happen. There is nothing wrong with girls playing rugby and they have as much talent as boys.

TEAM WORK TIPS

"How you interact off the pitch is just as important as how you are on the pitch. Team-building socials are a great way to get to know each other, and that is reflected on the pitch."
Harlequin Ladies Youth Academy.

"Remember to acknowledge your teammates' contributions when you have scored a try. There can't be anything worse that having a really good player in your team, but one that no one likes."
Richard Oliver, England.

"We have a high level of team spirit because we keep the boys together out of season by doing off season training (non rugby related).
Liverpool Collegiate RUFC U10s, winners of three tournaments.

"Rugby is an awesome sport to play. This season was the very first rugby season for my school and I only joined because I wanted to do something outrageous and crazy. It was crazy but I had a lot of fun. It is a team sport and you don't learn the true meaning of a team until you play the game and have experienced it for yourself."
Angelo B, Canada.

"The best teams are those who retain the ball and make fewer mistakes than everyone else. Don't neglect the basics in training! It is a bit of a kick in the teeth if your team makes 80m in a great running move only for you to knock it on and have the ball kicked back to your own 5m line."
Adam Clarke, Earlsdon RFC.

"I love rugby because it's the best form of venting any aggression or anger in a controlled and legal way; and I love the team playing aspect - having people watch your back and watching your team mates' backs. There's nothing that I don't like about being in the top 44. It's just sometimes hard to have to choose between being a bridesmaid at your best friend's wedding or playing for your country (ok, it's not a hard decision but it's hard letting friends and family down); rugby does take up most weekends and evenings but it is so worth it."
Sam Dale, England Students Hooker.

"To be the best you need quality training, to train as you mean to play, warm up before the game with 100% attitude as you can't do anything without commitment. Communicate during games so you know where to pass and off-load. To dig deep we always pull on past experience and our fitness levels both physically and mentally pull us through. The special qualities that our team has is team spirit and a will to want to play with each other.
St Mary's Old Boys RFC U13s, Gloucestershire Champions.

THE COACH DOCTOR

I'M HERE TO ANSWER ALL YOUR QUESTIONS

Hi Coachdoctor,
On Wednesday night my rugby team trained. We only had seven players. A few of our players from last season have quit. We don't have enough players. What can I do to help?
Geoff, aged seven, Belgium.

Dear Geoff,
The first thing I'm going to say is don't panic. Every team has to deal with low numbers at some point. No player is better than a team so don't worry, you can replace the players who have left. You can help by turning up for training every week. You could volunteer to design a leaflet to invite players to join the team and leave some leaflets in your local library or doctors. Another way you can help is by inviting some of your school mates to come along.
Coachdoctor

Hi Coachdoctor,
I've not been playing rugby for very long. Last
week our coach said there's a rugby festival
coming up. The problem is… I don't know what a
tournament is. Can you help?
Craig, aged nine, USA.

Dear Craig,
A rugby festival is another name for a rugby
tournament. Instead of playing one game like
normal you will play in several. You will
usually play three matches in a pool and then a
final. A pool is another word for a group. You
will probably be in a group with three other
teams. You'll play a match against each of them
and the scores will be added up. If you win the
most matches you will be in the final. If you
win the final you will get a medal and a trophy.
Rugby festivals are so much fun! You'll enjoy
them loads more than normal matches. You'll get
to play teams you've never played before.
Good luck,
Coachdoctor

School rugby is different from club rugby. It offers more challenges because players have a real mixture of rugby playing experience.

If you've never played before you might be a bit nervous about what to expect. Don't be. Relax. It'll be fine. In many ways school rugby is a much simpler game because the teams have only just been put together and lots of players will be picking up the oval ball for the first time. This means that the game plans will be a lot simpler and your coach will just want you to get the basics right.

If you've been playing club rugby you might find that you have to change positions when you play for your school team. Many towns have several rugby union and rugby league teams so when you start at secondary school your school team will have players from all the different teams as well as some new players. It might be that there are three budding scrumhalves who have played for their retrospective teams for years but at the end of the day only one can be on the pitch at one time.

<u>My Rugby Story</u>

At first I wanted to join rugby for the roughness of the sport and how it kinda resembled football, but now I see it differently. There is absolutely no other sport I prefer or love next to rugby. Rugby is more than just another team, it's like your 2nd family.

It was my first team sport I joined, and actually made the team, my position was number 8, and I was also one of our team captains. I was so proud of myself and was so excited to be apart of something so big, being it was our schools very first ever rugby team.

I had a goal set for myself, and that was to score a try, just one if possible. I ended up scoring our very first try, and followed with another 3. In rugby I wasn't the guy who didn't know what he was doing or the bad player, I was good, and this made me proud.

Adriano Rossi, Toronto, USA.

New team, new challenges

The first thing you need to do is learn everyone's name. It helps if you have some idea of who's played before and who hasn't. You won't have the support network that you had in your club team but over time you'll grow close as a team. It will take a few matches to get to know how your team mates play, who will be first to support you when you make a break, who's good at powering over, who's good at reading the game. Once you pick up on players strengths it will be a lot easier to win games. Try and help those players who have only just started playing. Be willing to put in more effort with them and help them outside of your school team training sessions. Maybe invite them to come to some of your club training sessions to give them more chance to practice.

Never let club rivalry affect your relationship with players in your school team. Pass to everyone, never refuse to include players because they play for the 'wrong' team. Sometimes this involves ignoring parents who constantly put down your team mates who play for the other side or code.

In school rugby you have to be more independent. In club rugby your parents watch all your games and take you to training. In school rugby many of the games take place in school time so you need to motivate yourself. You need to pack your own bag and turn up for every training session.

Commitment is important. You must never not turn up for a match when your team mates are depending on you. If you commit yourself to playing for the team you must play every match.

As a school team you might get the opportunity to play abroad. Rugby unites people of all races and you can play rugby virtually anywhere in the world.

THE COACH DOCTOR

I'M HERE TO ANSWER ALL YOUR QUESTIONS

Hi Coachdoctor,
Do you miss loads of lessons when you play for a school rugby team? When do you play the matches?
Cheers,
Hugh, aged eleven, Canada.

Dear Hugh,
Most schools play their matches after school finishes. They also train at least once a week so you need to commit to that too.
Coachdoctor

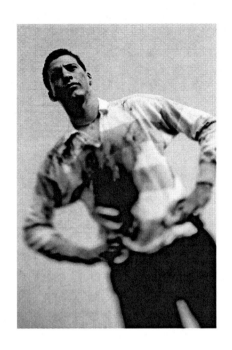

Hi Coachdoctor,
I'm thinking about playing rugby for my school
but I was wondering if you could tell me some of
the best things about school rugby.
From,
Shane, aged twelve, Australia.

Dear Shane,
Playing for your school team is simply the best!
You get to play against teams all across the
world. You'll probably go on tour…it's
fantastic. There are school cup competitions
too…with big prizes. You might get to meet your
favourite rugby players or play at a big stadium.
Give it a go, you won't be disappointed.
Coachdoctor

Hi Coachdoctor,
I want to be a professional rugby player so I
don't bother working at school. My friend says
I'm daft. what do you think?
Love from,
Paul, aged thirteen, England.

Dear Paul,
If you aren't trying at school you are going to
cause yourself problems in the future. You will
need a career after rugby. Start working at
school now before it's too late.
Coachdoctor

Chapter 6:

Rugby....Getting selected

This chapter is designed to prepare you for attending trials. By now you should have worked on your fitness, position skills and mental preparation. You have developed your skills and now it is down to the coaches to notice. Aside from reading this chapter please ask older players at your club or school what they experienced at the trials they've attended....they could give you vital information, like what the coaches are like or how long the trial lasts.

Getting Selected

There are no universal rules that coaches use when it comes to selection. Every coach is different. Getting selected by your regular coach is different from getting selected by your regional coach. Your regular club or school coach knows what you are like week in week out. They know what you are like at training and what sort of player you are. Regional coaches don't have this knowledge. You are lucky if they even know your name. Regional coaches pick their team from the trials they run. It is vital you give it your all at these trials. Let's look at getting selected at club/school level first then we'll look at getting picked at regional trials.

<u>Getting picked for your regular team:</u>

As we discussed in chapter 2, commitment and respect are important if you want to be the best. Another important thing is consistency. It is important that you perform at a high level all the time. There's no point being a player who can score a hat trick in one match but gets sent off in the next because things aren't going your way. Your coach is more likely to pick a player with less ability than you if he knows they will perform to a consistent level every match.

You have to be a team player to get selected. Too many young teams have the wrong idea and have one star player who scores all the tries. These teams might win but they will never be a great team. Great teams need great players who work together for their wins. If the star player gets injured or decides to switch to another team guess what happens...yep you guessed it the team folds. There's nothing wrong with enjoying scoring but you should be equally as happy when you give a good pass that results in someone else scoring.

<u>How parents can help:</u>

Don't tell your child they can have extra pocket money every time they score or that you'll buy them a present if they score a hat trick. Even though you mean well you are actually encouraging them to be selfish. Your child might even feel a bit of a failure even if the team wins...all because they didn't score a try.

It is important that you turn up for training and matches. It's surprising how many players reduce their chances of being selected again by failing to show up on match days. I'll give you an example:

The coach and team are in the changing room getting into their kit, talking through the set moves, waiting for Billy to turn up...and he doesn't show. Poor Alex has to step into Billy's position having never played a match before with only five minutes to go before kick-off. Because Billy was instrumental in the set moves the team can't use them. They lose the match.

If you can't make a match or training session ring your coach in advance. It's not acceptable to just not turn up or to ring five minutes before kick-off.

Being subbed

If you haven't been selected for a match or tournament think about what you need to improve on to make sure your selected next time. Be willing to ask your coach for tips and put in extra training sessions at home. Sometimes you have to be dropped from the team so that other players can have a turn. It's a fact of life and it happens to all players at some point. In tournaments teams can only have a set number of players so your coach might want to take you but can't because of team restrictions. Usually players can only play in a certain number of tournaments per season so don't expect to play every tournament.

Be prepared to be rested in some matches. Everyone hates being subbed half way through a match but your coach and team might need you to perform in a later match so might be subbing you to prevent you getting injured or over tired.

If you have just joined a team be prepared to be a sub for a few weeks. The coach isn't going to drop a committed member of the team so that you can appear in the starting line up. You have to earn your place. Cheer your team from the sidelines and watch every play so you learn more about each player and how the team works as a unit. Being the sub can actually be an advantage because you come on when everyone else is tired. This means you have more chances to shine and impress.

Getting picked at trials:

If you've never been to a trial you're probably wondering how you get picked to attend a trial. You can't simply turn up. It's usually up to your club or school coach to nominate you. Each coach is asked by the trial organisers to put forward the names of players who they think have the ability and attitude to be in the regional teams. Your club or school coach then has to think long and hard about who would be suited to be in a regional team. They might put forward two names, five names or fifteen names, it all depends on the quality of the team they coach. They won't put forward anyone just for the sake of it. If they did they'd be wasting the trial organisers time and the players time. A player who is not good enough will be left feeling demoralised if he is put forward to trials and struggles with everything he is asked to do at the trial.

The first step to getting picked at trials is to get nominated to attend the trial.

My rugby story

My name is Jamie George and I play for Saracens Academy, England u16s, England u18s and I was captain of London and South-East as a hooker.

I would love to say something about trials, seeing as at my first county trial, I didn't get in and then later that year I got another trial and ended up captaining the side and moving on from there!

Trials are times of supreme nerves, and a time that needs complete focus. It is often the case that trials are a lottery and having experienced many in my time, you need to do something that sticks out. Make yourself better and different from the other players around you. The key is to be loud and confident and make sure that people know you are there! It is such an often occurrence that sometimes the best players don't stick out and hide in other people's shadows, don't be one of those people.

Everyone deserves to have the chance and you must realise that not getting in the first time isn't the end of the world, you need to keep going and never quit, and your chances will come! Rugby is a game of skill, but is probably the most rewarding game of all!

How trials are run

There are two main ways a trial is run.

The first way is through a series of trial games. The second way is by a number of drills and exercises followed by a short match.

You won't usually know which type of trial is used until you get there. That's why it's a good idea to talk to older players in your club or school and ask them what the trial was like when they attended. This extra knowledge will help you mentally prepare for the trial before you get there. It will also help you schedule in some trial specific training sessions in the weeks leading up to the trial.

Trial type 1: A series of trial games.

For this type of trial you usual turn up in your rugby kit and have to find a notice board with the trial teams and match schedule. You might be in a team with some players you know or you may be with complete strangers. You should know at least a couple of players in your trial team, whether they're team mates or people you've played against.

Right before your first match you'll probably be feeling a bit sick. That's normal. All rugby players find themselves under pressure at some point. It will probably take a few minutes into the game for you to get back to normal.

Organisation is always lacking from the teams put together at trials. Players bunch together instead of spreading out which results in tempers getting frayed and lots of dropped balls. Players often fail to support and everyone fights to be the one who receives the ball. This is normal and the selectors know this.

To make yourself stand out from the rest you have to be different. Yes you want to get your hands on the ball but you want to show the selectors that you can contribute to the team in different ways. For instance, in rugby union, you might drive over again and again, winning the ball for your team. In rugby league, you might put in tackle after tackle, putting pressure on the opposition. Try and be involved with every play, you won't get noticed if you're not there. Above all you have to beat your opposite number at everything. If you are fullback then it is your goal to be better than all the fullbacks at the trial...that is who the selectors are judging you against.

It is important that you have a professional attitude at trials. The selectors will be walking around and watching how players behave off the field. Trials are not places to mess around and have a laugh. If one of your team mates from school is stood next to you pulling faces and talking daft then you need to make your excuses and move. You don't want the selectors to think you are like that.

Have you got Captain qualities?

Every team needs a leader and trial teams are no different. If you are good at reading the games don't be afraid to direct others. Good leaders help teams win. Some players need direction. They need encouragement to push harder in mauls or to get to the breakdown to drive over (rugby union). At goal line drop outs your team needs to cover every possibility so tell players where to stand (rugby league).

The selectors will notice the impact you are making to the team.

If you normally play rugby union but you are attending a rugby league trial or vice versa you can still succeed. Many of the skills are the same. You do need to have watched the code you are playing at the trial and know the basics. It will take a few minutes to get used to playing the ball or setting the ball but soon it should become second nature. The selectors will recognise your raw ability.

Trial type 2: Drills, exercises and a short match

In many ways this is the tougher of the two different types of trials. Many players who are great in matches fail to be selected because their passing and catching skills are not up to scratch. There is one simple answer to this problem and that is practice your passing and catching every day. Get good at it. It can seem impossible for some players but everyone can improve their passing and catching techniques if they put the time and effort in. You don't need to be the best passer in your team but you have to make sure that when you're doing drills and exercises at the trial you aren't the player who drops the ball every time. The players who drop the ball during drills and exercises are usually the players who have problems with concentration.

Improving your concentration skills:

The same drill can sometimes last half an hour. This is immensely boring but you just have to keep on going. You can't stop and take a water break half way through a drill. This messes everyone up and shows a lack of commitment on your part.

The match at the end of the trial is usually over within twenty minutes. Although you'll enjoy this part of the trial the most it is important that you've performed well in the drills and exercises. The selector needs to be able to tick every box. You need to be a good all round rugby player.

Trials are usually two hours long which is a lot longer than the average training session. You will benefit greatly from the extra sessions you have been doing as part of your fitness planner. Players who don't put in the time off the rugby field often struggle in the last half an hour of the trial. They simply run out of energy.

Trials are not as interesting as normal training sessions and in no way are they supposed to be fun. The coaches at trials are trying to push you to your limit to see who can keep on going. Experienced coaches know how demanding regional matches are and so want players who can last the full eighty minutes. It is harder to get into a regional side than a club side because it is the next step, you are raising your game to another level.

What next?

If the trial selectors were impressed with your trial you will usually receive a letter in the post or the team will be announced on the regional website. If you have been selected this is great news and you deserve a pat on the back. Quite often though you are only through the first trial and you may have to attend a couple more trials before you make the full team.

If you haven't been selected please don't be discouraged. At trials there are sometimes eighty players all competing for twenty places. The selectors have a lot of players to see and sometimes they don't have enough time to see everyone for a great length of time.

Even if you don't make it this time remember your club or school coach thinks you have what it takes. You've still beaten some players who didn't get nominated to go to the trial in the first place.

The "It's not fair Tom Munson got picked and I didn't" problem

No one likes not getting picked but sometimes the worst thing is that someone else from our club or school team gets picked. We feel cheated and jealous. Parents are sometimes just as bad and will often ring your club coach to moan. They want the club coach to agree with them , that "Tom Munson" isn't as good a player as their child. This is completely the wrong thing to do. Instead of ringing your coach to moan you should be ringing Tom Munson to congratulate him. It is something worth celebrating when anyone in your team does well.

Remember it's not Tom Munson's fault that he got picked and you didn't. Maybe Tom Munson is a prop and you play scrumhalf. At trials you are being compared to other players who play in your position not all players.

Trial selectors are only human and they make mistakes. Sometimes they make the wrong decisions. A small majority will select someone because their granddad was a famous rugby player or because they know the players dad. It is very frustrating when they do that! You shouldn't let this get you down. If they want to cheat and let someone who isn't good enough get into the team then they'll pay the price on match day. This won't carry on forever. A team can only carry a player so far. In a year's time when there's a new trial selector they won't get picked.
At the end of the day if you have the talent to make it in rugby you will. There are always other trials. You can focus you attention on making it next time.

GETTING SELECTED TIPS

"Selection is always a contentious subject, not all coaches look for the same attributes in a player. Work hard in training and do your best at all times, we can't ask anymore as coaches if you give 100%."
Ray Harris, North Lancashire Coach.

"Always get the first hit in on your opposing player and ensure they know who won that encounter!"
Simon Pape, Andover RFC U9s Coach.

"Your ball handling ability is so important, it doesn't matter how fast or strong you are if you can't pass or catch the ball you won't get selected at county trials. A player who is neither very strong or very fast can stand out if he has great hands."
Paul Lewis, Wallasey RUFC Manager.

"When I was at Leeds there were camps, like area, then Yorkshire and then England. I went to the Leeds camp and you had to get through that to go to the Yorkshire camp but they said I wasn't good enough, but I thought no way. I kept trying my best and I ended up getting picked for England and there was me and one other lad who didn't get through to Yorkshire camp but ended up playing for England because we were good enough."
Jason Golden, Wakefield Wildcats.

"If you make a mistake, it's done - put it behind you. Focus on the next play and not what happened before. When you do well, enjoy the feeling and the crediting from your team mates, it's that feeling you want again and again!"
Nigel Godolphin Youth Chairman for Camberley RFC.

"Have a mental belief in your own ability."
Stuart Braley, St Mary's Old Boys U13s Coach.

"The best young players have a real inner confidence and granite like determination to overcome and succeed coupled with a quick brain that 80 -90% of the time takes the right option, this gives them that extra yard they appear to have more time. Add in enormous athletic and physical ability and you have a potential international player."
Gus Hellier,Saffron Walden RFC Fitness Coach.

"Rugby is a physical game, but a player with a bad attitude never succeeds. Matches are more often won and lost in the mind than on the pitch"
Simon Bates, Windsor Rugby Youth Chairman.

"When you are training and playing, you need to possess that extra bit of will power that says "I CAN keep going."
Tamara Taylor, England International Second Rower.

"Support and motivate others to improve on their weaknesses."
Stephen Coppin, Trafford MV U8s Assistant Coach.

"Always train hard. Remember it's what you do when no ones watching that matters. You need to be confident, never let anyone write you off, no matter who they are. Being a smaller player I've been written off by many so called know it alls but I never let it shake me."
Ryan Manyika, Zimbabwe U19s and Harlequins.

"Attitudes and behaviours are so important if you want to be a great rugby player - skills and decision making can be learned, physical fitness achieved but belief, mental toughness, commitment to team mates, awareness of self and work ethic are priceless."
Amanda Bennett, Head Coach Saracens and England A.

"Do the basics well under pressure. Play with your head up so you can see what is happening so you can react to situations as they develop when defending, or shape the game when in attack Do not overcomplicate the game - my favourite backs move is to make four passes - this normally ends in a try and does not involve 'moves' that usually go wrong!"
Andy Smith, Chairman of Dorset & Wiltshire Coaching Committee.

THE COACH DOCTOR

I'M HERE TO ANSWER ALL YOUR QUESTIONS

Hi Coachdoctor,
I've fell out with my parents. They don't understand me. We're going as a family to Florida for two weeks and I don't want to go anymore. There's a trial for my regional team while we're away. My parents say I have to go on holiday with them.
Love
Bethany, aged fourteen, Scotland.

Dear Bethany,
I'm afraid you're not going to like this...I think your parents are right. Your parents have paid a lot of money for your holiday and you need to go. There are always other trials. Your coach might be able to speak to the regional coach and see if you can try out when you get back.
Coachdoctor

Hi Coachdoctor,
I haven't been picked for a tournament but I
still want to help my team win. Have you got any
ideas how I can help them?
From,
Daniel, aged seven, South Africa.

Dear Daniel,
It is fantastic that you want to help your team.
You can help at training by trying your best when
you have a practice match. This will help them
because they will have to work harder. You can
also help on match day by carrying the water
bottles and cheering from the sidelines.
Coachdoctor

Chapter 7:

Rugby.... The next step

Things get really exciting once you are in a county team. You are climbing higher on the rugby ladder. There will be important people watching your games to see if you have what it takes to play for your country.

<u>County/regional sides</u>

If you are successful in your trials you will make it to into your county or regional squad. The hard work really begins then. Usually you are picked to join a county or regional squad of forty or so players. The squad is then divided into an A and a B team after a few training sessions or a weekend training camp. Obviously everyone wants to be in the A team but it takes a lot of skill and effort to make it. If you are put in the B team do your best to push for a promotion to the A team. Show the selectors your class through the training exercises and during matches.

As you move up the rugby ladder there is more pressure to do well. You have to give it everything, if you are only on the field for ten minutes then you have to perform to the best standard you can. You have the ability to change matches. For instance if your team loses 30 points to 10 but were losing 30 points to nil points when you came on with twenty minutes to go then you might have stopped your team getting thrashed even more. You might have scored the try or provided the pass which the person scored off. If you perform well in the time your regional coach gives you on the pitch then in the next match you might be in the starting line-up or have more time.

England Students Rugby League Team

The best county and regional teams are the teams that gel. Sometimes you play county teams from different countries which is a test in itself as sometimes they have started their regional or county sides a couple of years before yours was set up. This is a great advantage because the players all know each other and know how they all play. There is nothing you can do about this. You just have to try and quickly learn how players in your own team operate. You've got to try and dominate your opposite number and make sure you are better player. Rugby matches are battles and the team that has the most mental and physical toughness will win.

Sometimes the regional or county coach may ask you to play in a different position from the position you usually play. You have to embrace this and do all you can to learn the skills required for this position. There's no point sulking and refusing to change, if you do that you'll find yourself dropped. If your coach asks you to change position at a training session by the next training session you need to be up to speed. At county and regional level the coaches have limited training sessions so they can't afford to wait around. You need to put in the hours practicing in your own time.

Set moves and calls

Every team has different names for different moves. Teams also do different set moves. For instance a scissors pass may be called PSP, S or Wilko depending on which team you play for. Your team will have unique names for moves so that other teams don't understand what you are planning. County and regional teams are no different. If you are given a sheet of paper with twenty moves and their code names on, you need to make sure that you know them all off by heart. You need to learn them otherwise you are holding your new team back.

Top tips for learning code names

When you get home it's a good idea to copy the moves and names onto a large sheet of paper. You will find colour coding and using images will help you remember. Don't bombard yourself by trying to learn all the names at once. Divide them up into manageable groups. It's much easier if you learn all the moves from the scrum together, all the moves from the kick-off together, all the moves from a penalty together and so on. It is easier to remember things when they appear during your everyday routine too. Why not stick a copy on your fridge or on the bathroom door. If your family are willing to help ask them to test you. To prepare yourself for the match situation get them to test you when you are already doing something, i.e. practicing passing and catching. Your mind will be concentrating on catching the ball but will have to answer at the same time. If you think about the answer too much you will drop the ball. By the time you go training again you will be able to recall the set moves and calls easily without making a mistake.

What's next?

If you have the ability and talent to be a professional player you will be noticed by the big clubs. They will want to sign you for their Academy team. Don't panic if you don't get signed straight away. Don't think that you have to choose between going to college/university or playing for a club. You can usually do both and the rugby club will support you in your studies. It is good to have qualifications to fall back on.

Once you are in an Academy side you have to make sure you keep working. You have to use the Academy training sessions and matches to show the coaches that you are ready for a first team place. It will take time and there will be many setbacks but don't lose heart.

Remember to be professional at all times and recognise that if you don't work hard your club might drop you. The best Academy players will move on to the first team and may even play for their country. Good luck!

Thank you

A big thank you to the following players, coaches and teams:

Fred Ahern,

Mahdin Al-Benghalee,

Nathan Alexander,

Lee Allen,

Anthony Amoratis,

Matt Arden,

Mark Ashworth,

Geoff Ball,

Rick Barrow,

Chris Barry,

Sam Batterton,

Simon Bates,

Yvonne Baxter,

Nick Betts,

Ian Biglin,

Chris Bluer,

Branden Bolton,

Stuart Braley,

Janessa Brouilette-Culliford,

Ignacio Browne,

James Broxton,

Luke Bugden,

John Bullen,

Christina Bunce,

Justin Burnell,

Callum Busfield,

Gareth Campbell,

Leah Carey,

Matthew Chapman,

Adam Clarke,

Calum Clark,

Joe Clark,

Joe Clarke,

Jordan Combden,

Jumbles Cook,

Kirsten Cook,

Geoff Cooke,

Stephen Coppin,

Steve Cowman,

Richard Coskie,

Joseph Cowley,

Jason Critchley,

Scott Critchley,

Steve Cullen,

Sam Dale,

Jonathan Dance,

Jonathan Davidson

Suzanne Davidson,

Sue Day,

April Del Zotto,

Anthony Dennison,

Stuart Dodds,

Aaron Duggan,

Tom Dugarin,

Chris Dunham,

Trevor Edwards,

Edward English,

Peter Elder,

Arthur Ellis,

Jeff Fell,

Zach Fenoglio,

Gaspar Firmat,

Sebastian Fish,

Erin Fitzpatrick,

Kyle Foliey,

Rob Fonterigo,

John Foster,

Robert Fox,

Catherine Gardner,

Adam Geoghegan,

Jamie George,

Kevin George,

Jason Golden,

Alex Goodhew,

Jonathan Gray,

Adam Greendale,

Ron Hall,

Ray Harris,

Gavin Hatton,

Lewis Hawkins,

Bryan Hayes,

Claire Hines,

Louis Hinshelwood,

Spencer Hodgins,

Pete Howard,

Sarah Hunter,

Seb Jewell,

Colin Johnson,

Derek Johnston,

Mike Jones,

Ben Jonson,

Remy Julienne,

Chad Kerina,

James Kinsella,

Zachery Klima,

Tiffany Koivu,

Marky Komar,

Charles Lang,

Matty Lancaster,

Emma Layland,

Donny LeVasseur,

Edward Lewis,

Brandon Lillico,

Eddie Lloyd,

Sean Maher,

Max Malkin,

Rebecca Mallinder

Ryan Manyika,

Susy Marriott,

Spencer Matthews,

Marc Mauntel,

Caleb Mazaika,

Jo McGilchrist,

Bert McGaughey,

Peter McGuiness,

Peter McIntee,

David McLaughlin,

Tim Medici,

Ben Mercer,

Jen Miller,

Steve Mills,

Joe Millson,

Mike Minervini,

Kendra Moore,

Sean Moran,

Alasdair Muller,

Matthew Murtagh-Wu,

Daniel Musto,

Jesse Neufeld,

Camilla Nicolson,

Dan Oliver,

Derek Oliver,

Harry Oliver,

Jane Oliver,

Liz Oliver,

Richard Oliver,

Jim O'Neill,

Clarke O'Reilly,

Arthur Osano,

Yoram Ouanounou,

Peter Owens,

Amanda Philips,

Frankie Pinder,

Henry Edwards,

Mickeal du Plessis,

Joe Polakovic,

Callum Potter,

Sean Quinn,

Shelley Rae,

Zach Remez,

Gareth Reynolds,

Georgina Roberts,

Sam Roberts,

Adriano Rossi,

Mark Robinson,

Nina Roe,

Joseph Russell,

Claire Sanderson,

Nick Saunders,

Keith Scarratt,

Tom Scott,

Nathan Seggie,

Johann Serfontein,

Steven Shenkman,

Alan Smith,

Andy Smith,

Max Smith,

Tony Smith,

Michaela Staniford,

Georgia Stevens,

Chris Stewart,

Fred Stonehouse,

Katy Storie,

Josh Stump,

Jon Symons,

Tamara Taylor,

Kerry Attwell Thomas,

Matthew Thomas,

Matt Tichias,

Richard Timms,

Jordan Tisdale,

Bob Turner,

Dave Turner,

Steve Viezel,

Susie Walker,

John Welsh,

Charlotte West,

Phil Westren,

James White,

Peter White,

Lauren Whitelock,

Joe Wilburn,

Helen Williams,

John Williams,

Rosie Williams,

Tom Wilson,

Chad Wright,

Morgan Yeroschak.

Teams

Widnes RUFC u13s,

Wakefield Trinity Wildcats,

St Marys Old Boys RFC u13s,

Crawley RFC,

Widnes RUFC,

North Dorset girls,

Aldwinians u14s,

Tynedale Panthers,

Basfordlow u17s,

Letchworth Garden City girls,

Harlequin Ladies Youth Academy,

Widnes u7s,

Liverpool Collegiate,

L'Amoreaux C.I,

Cornish Pirates.

A special thanks to the RFUW and PremierRugby.

Bibliography

Bath, Richard, *The complete guide to rugby union* (Carlton, 2003).

Briscowe, Tony, *Rugby- Steps to Success* (Human Kinetics, Oxford, 1998).

Cain, Nick, *Rugby union for dummies* (John Wiley, 2004).

Wedd, Kerry, *Heading for the top-rugby for ambitious young players* (Quiller Press, London, 1997).

www.rfu.com

www.nz.com

www.rugbyworld.com

www.scrum.com

www.rugbycamps.co.uk

www.huddersfieldrl.co.uk

www.superleague.com

If you ever want to learn more or need some more inspiration try reading the extra quotes below.

"Everyone has their own style when playing rugby no matter what position they play, just try to express yourself when playing rugby."
Mat Tichias, England Lionhearts RL.

"Just because you're a forward don't think you can't pass or kick. Rather than just driving the ball in, look to pass it if someone's in a better position. Don't just think you can't kick or pass."
Jason Golden, Wakefield Wildcats.

"I've had to face rejection. When I was playing for England u16s I was dropped and then recalled and then dropped again. I went to have a starting place at England u18s a year young."
Peter Elder, Wasps.

"Get out of your comfort zone. If you always play at a level you are comfortable at and not challenged by, you will never improve."
Calum Clark, Leeds Tykes Academy.

"In training never accept anything less than my best, 4 out of 5 is not good enough as the 5th one may be crucial in a match. At fly half as a young player try things, run, and kick. Don't be one dimensional."

Adam Greendale, Leed Tykes Academy.

"No one is perfect so we can all learn something."
Stuart Gilbert, Army U23s.

"I am a big guy at 6'5" 270 and my biggest challenge was just getting the nerve to go out and run on my own and getting in great shape. Once you get over the first week it comes naturally."
Jeffrey Fell, USA U17s.

"To prepare for a big match I find the biggest person on my team and practice tackling so I don't screw up on the day."
Bryan Hayes, University of Cincinnati RFC.

"Visualisation is always good, especially for kickers. "
Peter McIntee, Ashton on Mersey.

"I prepare for big matches by stretching and saying a prayer. I always personally say a quick prayer for my team and for myself; that whatever happens, we will play our best and won't get too hurt."
Vladimir, Cambridge Rindge and Latin Falcons team.

"You should push yourself to your limits

but don't do anything stupid, like starting weights at too young an age."
Eduard Lewis, Buckinghamshire County U17s.

My greatest rugby moment was winning Player of the Tournament at the national schools festival. I had played at the same tournament two years earlier and had thought then that I'd never be able to adjust to the level I'd seen that day. To go on a couple of years to win the player of the tournament meant a lot to me."
Ryan Manyika, Zimbabwe U19s and Harlequins.

"You need to practice the basic skills, i.e. passing and being able to kick from both feet, even if you don't play in a position that requires these skills. By practicing these things you will become a better player."
Seb Jewell, Harlequins and England U21s.

"The challenge that I have had to overcome is a lack of confidence. As a new player playing with experienced ruggers, I had a tendency to hang back during practices and games, afraid that I would do something wrong. I had

to realize that I was never going to improve that way, and would ALWAYS be hanging back if I took that attitude. I'm working on overcoming that, and fully participating to the best of my ability so that I can learn and master new rugby skills.
Amanda Philips, Harvard Women's Rugby Team.

"I was told I was too small to be a hooker at a high level. I proved them wrong when I played for Devon at Twickenham."
Sam Roberts, South West U18s.

"Before every game when I was sixteen, playing in the school 1st XV I kicked balls back and forth to my mum in my conservatory, about 100 on each foot in the morning before, when it was 2pm kick off."
Tom Dugarin, King's College School.

"I sprained my medial ligament three times and tore it. I believed my rugby dreams were over, I attended physio and continued building up my strength in my knee, until I could play again. It was a slow process with many set backs but now I'm playing the best rugby of my life. I've been picked for England Students and I'm hoping to win the National Cup with Leeds Met Rugby Union Team."
Elizabeth Oliver, England Students Rugby League Team.

"Don't worry about going in for tackles against people who are running at full pace. The fastest they run at you, the harder they fall."
Lauren Whitelock, Marlow RFC Ladies.

"Practice, throw a ball around with a few mates, and devise fun training games - if you find a week area in your skills base, work on it with guidance if necessary until it becomes a strength rather than a weakness"
Alasdair Muller, King's School Canterbury.

"I find knowing the rules helps. So either help coach a high school team or junior team. You could even referee junior games."
Nathan Alexander Pratt, St John Labatt Trojans RFC.

"Being a winger isn't all about the big run. You have to keep your feet in contact and run with your support. There will be games were you don't see the ball much. As short side wing, run the inside angle with your centre and fullback, always giving them two options. Make sure you can always catch the ball at top speed."

Nathan Alexander Pratt, St John Labatt Trojans RFC.

"I was in the team and things were going good and then I hurt my ribs and couldn't train and I found that quite hard but John Kear my coach said keep working hard and there's a place for you in the team. Once my ribs got better I took my chance and played six games in a row."
Jason Golden, Wakefield Wildcats.

"I just switched clubs and the biggest challenge was earning respect once again and showing the coach I was able to play with starters. I always make sure I'm the first at training and the last to leave."
Gaspar Firmat, Chile.

Pass the ball through your hands as much as possible, always be confident and run straight.
Max Smith, Sedbergh School.

"Don't back down from a tackle even if you can't take the guy down you will slow him down until someone else can."
Mickeal du Plessis, Rideau High School.

"I taught a bunch of Swedes at our school what rugby was and in two months got that school team to compete in the U19 Youth National

Championships with clubs. We're doing pretty well, we may still win it. We entered an international school tournament for rugby, the first time our school had ever been represented in a tournament of rugby...and won it, convincingly. Now a year later many of the team are playing for Sweden at an international level."
Sebastian Fish, Sigtuna Exiles.

"You'll never feel the rush if you don't take the risk."
Spencer, Pearson High School

One of our greatest victories was this years Gloucestershire Cup Final. From the moment I woke up that morning I just had a vibe and the thought of us winning. Then before kick- off the vibe got stronger as our pre-match warm up and preparation was fantastic. Then as the game progressed every player put every thing into the game. We ended up winning the match with some outstanding play."
St Mary's Old Boys RFC U13s, Gloucestershire Champions.

"In mini tag rugby, games are won by forcing the other team to make mistakes. Keep up the pressure, gain the advantage be winning the loose ball, or forcing the

opposing team into touch."
Widnes RUFC U7s.

"The biggest challenge I had to get over was not being selected for Yorkshire U15's. I made sure that I was better prepared for the U16 season. I went on to become England U16 Captain."
Adam Greendale, England U19.

"The players that stand out are the players that are strong mentally. You have to have the right mental attitude and have mental strength. Ability is not enough on its own if you want to be a professional player."
Jason Critchley, Former Welsh International.

"I play basketball in my back garden and this helps me keep supple and makes my jumping better. I also play basketball for my school team."
Jon Green, Bredon Buzzards.

"To improve my game at home I live with a rugby ball in my hands, play football with a rugby ball and even basket ball with a rugby ball. I also try and stay fit by going running and cycling most days. I make sure I am getting the right food for me to grow, stay strong, and keep fit. At home after a game it is important for me to rest."

Will Graulich, Bredon Buzzards.

"When you step out on the pitch think about your team, your family...never forget the community you represent."
Sean Moran, America.

"Never hesitate before making a tackle. If you hesitate that's when you'll get hurt."
Clarke O'Reilly, America.

"What happens on the rugby pitch stays on the rugby pitch. You can battle with someone during the match but afterwards you'll shake hands and respect one another."
Arthur Osano, England.

"I've been lucky enough to play at Twickenham with my school team. When you're playing, you are in the match mode and focused. You have objectives and goals...whether it is in your back garden or in an 80,000 seater stadium."
James Kinsella, England.

"The night before I just try and keep my mind off the game and see my mates that I know away from rugby. I'll go on the computer or something and just chill out."
Jason Golden, Wakefield Wildcats.

"You can achieve your goals. I wanted to

play in the RFU County Championship for NLD but I hadn't played rugby for three years. I wanted it so badly that I trained four times a week for two years...and this summer I achieved my goal. If you want it, go for it."
Rick Barrow, England.

"Don't let the rough times tear you down. Use the insults to make you a stronger and tougher player."
Mike Minervini, England.

"If you are thinking about playing rugby for the first time, give it a try. Although rugby may have the appearance that it is a tough, brutal sport, don't let that get to you. You could be such a great player...just see where it can take you."
Kirsten Marie Cook, America.

"When you get the ball you have ten seconds of fame and fifteen reasons not to run, but you do...and that's what makes you great at the sport."
Mickeal Du Plessis, America.

"Just go all out, there is nothing better than to play the game and fall in love with it. I did and I never regretted a moment of it. The rush of playing is amazing and will never get old.
Marc Mauntel, America.

"I remember my first game. We were the city boys and we were facing the farm boys. There hadn't been a rugby team in our school for over ten years. We were all rookies in the game, I thought it was pretty crazy. It was a tough, physical match and even though we lost it was still a good game."
Mahdin Al-Benghalee, America.

"Always tackle low, around the knees is the best spot. If you learn to play properly you should be able to avoid serious injuries."
Nathan Seggie, America.

"Rugby is more than just a sport where you bang each other around, it is a lifestyle."
Ignacio Brown, Africa.

"I remember my first game being a very big blur. It was an odd sensation as it seemed to a massive free for all! I hardly remember seeing the ball. It was only sometime later, after a few more matches that I realised that actually the game is very organised and disciplined. It is a thinking game, rather than the bonkers game I first thought it was."
Susie Walker, England.

"Going out and playing rugby was the best decision I ever made. Everyone else who I've ever convinced to try out

and play has LOVED the sport and stuck with it ever since. I personally went from being one of the most clueless, shy and tiniest players on my team to eventually the most valuable player and one of the best rugby players in the region. My advice? Don't let anyone doubt you and don't be intimidated. It's a great sport and starting to play will probably the best decision you'll ever make."
April Del Zotto, America.

"Watch for those no. 8's picking up the ball behind the scrum.....especially near the try line....the last thing you want is to be caught off guard at that part of the field."
Chris Dunham, Canada.

"When you're marking your man, watch the overlap. Don't get too distracted. Watch your man, because if he does an overlap and you didn't see it coming you're in trouble."
Mahdin Al-Benghalee, America.

"Remember to acknowledge your teammates' contributions when you have scored a try. There can't be anything worse that having a really good player in your team, but one that no one likes."

Richard Oliver, England.

"The best advice I can give from a players perspective is that: To be successful on the field, you have to work your butt off when your off the field, training is the key to success, especially in the fast paced world of rugby."
Nick Betts, America.

"The best piece of wisdom I got from a rugby coach. He said that after almost thirty years coaching the game, I have realised how to play it. Get the ball and run at the gap between the two men, not AT the men, you'll be far more successful that way."
Bert McGaughey, London.

"Break your nose not your neck- in the scrum if it ever collapses keep your face foward its better to fall on your face and break your nose then to turn your head and break your neck."
Anthony Amoratis, America.

"Your brain is the most important tool on the field, don't use it against yourself."
TJ Jarvis, America.

"The second your opponent doubts his ability is the moment he gets either angry or desperate, both will usually end in mistakes which you can then capitalize on

Tom Scott, Canada.

"If you want to be the best and become a professional player one day you need to embrace extra practice and not avoid difficult activities and fitness training."
Josh Stump, Canada.

"My coach is Denis Sarazen and he was a Canadian international. He has taught me so much about rugby. Our school team is so successful because of the way he's pushed us. In practice when people won't run anymore he shouts "If you're not tired RUN! If you ARE tired RUN HARDER!""
Mickeal Du Plessis, America.

"I didn't start playing until I was twenty four so I had a step learning curve to get into the team. I'm a second rower and I learnt early on that you're only useful if you're at every ruck and maul, and actually doing something when you get there. This is exhausting because when you're not running, you're pushing and when you're not pushing, you're driving...you're constantly on the move. If you're not fit that it's impossible to do well."
Fred Ahern, England.

"If you ever get injured or hurt never show the

pain. Don't let the opposition know they have hurt you."
Fred Stonehouse, Italy.

"I've only been playing for a little while but my top tip is that you should go to every team practice. Practice is the most important part."
Louis Alexander Hinshelwood, Canada.

"Rugby players have a huge respect for the game and a huge respect for their opponent. It takes courage to walk onto the pitch and put your body through everything that a rugby game entails, this is without pads, timeouts, or subs, so it always warmed my heart to see how respectful rugby athletes are to each other after a match."
Joe P,America.

"I played in England and wasn't very good but I moved to the USA and I've developed so much. I've even had trials for the national side. I want to tell you to never give up. You can do it!
Joe Cowley, America.
"Don't be a ball hog. People think that they need to hold on to the ball and run a few people over to get noticed, but in the process they only hurt the team and make themselves look bad."
Steven Shenkman, England.

"Give it everything on the pitch. Remember pain is temporary but glory lasts forever."
Zach Remez, Canada.

"At trials talk to other people around you, as a selector is more likely to pick you if you look like a team player. Never argue with the ref, take out your frustrations on the opposition with powerful hits that are LEGAL. Don't high tackle though, it's dangerous and you could get sent off."
Charlotte West, England.

"Defence is so important. If you need inspiration, look towards the likes of Lee Radford, Jamie Peacock and Lee Gilmour who play in the Super League. They are not players who stand out but they are all giants in defence and you only notice them when they're not playing. They go out and do a job, nothing fancy, just hard, solid work."
Matthew Chapman, England.

"Hesitation will be any players downfall. Have confidence and play until you hear the whistle."
Jen Stone, Canada.

"Rugby is an awesome sport to play. This season was the very first rugby season for my school and I only joined because I wanted to do something outrageous and crazy. It was crazy but I had a lot of fun. It is a team sport and you don't learn the true meaning of a team until you play the game and have experienced it for yourself."
Angelo B, Canada.

"The advice I'd give second rowers is when jumping at the lineout, after catching the ball hold the ball just for a second or so rather than flicking it on straight away - gives you time to look down to see where the scrum half is and make sure the pass down is pinpoint."
Anthony Dennison, England.

"Tell your goal to the person who doesn't think you can make it. Prove them wrong."
Sean Maher, England.

"Rugby is so much more a team game than any other team sport. Each position has its own responsibilities and coaches know what to expect from each position. Therefore a great way of getting noticed is to do your own job well, and then be ready to support the rest of the team to do theirs."
Phil Stockbridge, Burton U15s Coach.

"Natural ability helps you become a great player. This has to be tapped by good coaching but a good coach can only make progress with players who are keen to learn and are willing to concentrate."
Brandon Cook, Burton RFC Coach.

"As a Centre I developed the ability to draw and give the ball prior to, during and after a tackle. Keep the ball available, run in such a way as to create space for others."
Jez Michaels, Kent Society Referee.

"Young players should always have lots of breaks for water during training as they do not store water in the same way as older children and adults. Older children and adults should always build in the warm down period into their training which will help the muscles and the heart."
Derek Johnston, Mini Chairman for New Milton and District RFC.

"Make sure you have an early night before the game otherwise you will struggle with concentration and energy."
Collin Johnson, Widnes RUFC U7s Coach.

"Don't cheat, you may think that you are beating your coach by doing fitness training half hearted i.e. miscounting when doing press ups etc but

in the long term you only cheat yourself."
Richard Timms, Bolton U13s Coach.

"As a former 'winger' the best view to this position is 'death or glory', you have to be totally committed to your run, almost get tunnel vision and not to worry about that big hairy prop or second row who's coming at full speed to stop you from scoring either by a bone crunching tackle of by being hit into touch so hard you still feel it 3 days later!"
Richard Timms, Bolton U13s Coach.

"Ultimately a "great" team in terms of trophies will need many good players, team spirit, time to train and a good coach. Teams lacking in the playing talent can still reach above themselves and whist not winning trophies etc are still "great" in my opinion."
Mark Robinson, Bolton RUFC U12s Coach.

"If you want to be the best you'll need two things: commitment and aggression."
Peter McGuinness, Sedgley Park U15s Coach.

"Make sure all your muscles are warm before and after exercise."
Gavin Hatton, Widnes RUFC Colts Scrum Half.

"Have pride in yourself and a determined mindset. Watch older players in your position to learn early some good habits. Copy that older player and ask questions of that player or your coach to help you apply new aspects to your game."
Jim O'Neill, Widnes RUFC Chairman of Rugby.

"Swim or cycle, especially in the summer."
Kerry Attwell Thomas, Andover U13s Coach.

"Set yourself goals or targets, short and long term and measure your success. Use the results to redefine your goals. Do not be afraid of failing but when you do analyse why they got more points than you and set about improving those areas."
John Welsh, New Milton Coach.

"Drink water, eat fruit and vegetables with your meat. Stay off fast food."
David McLaughlin Convenor, London Scottish Minis.

"Pick one thing to concentrate on each week and just practice that - try and do too much and you'll end up frustrated."
Camilla Nicholson, Basingstoke Ladies 1st XV Scrum Half.

"Try things, don't play safe."
Peter White, New Milton RFC Colts Coach.

"Eat sensibly on festival days...it's amazing how many parents send their kids along with choccy, crisps and fizzy drinks."
John Bullen, New Milton Rugby Club U8s Coach.

"Find something you're good at whether it be skill, work-rate or determination and make that be the key to your game. When you find it make sure you're the best at it. For me it's my work-rate and dedication and I know when I'm on the field I'm confident there's no one trying harder than me."
Jason Golden, Wakefield Wildcats.

"Prepare yourself psychologically... some players need to be aroused, some players need to be relaxed...it's important to know which works for you."
John Foster, Liverpool St Helens RUFC Chairman of the Junior Rugby Section.

"Eat little and often, particularly before a game. It assists your energy levels, performance and digestion. Manage injuries properly. I didn't and pay the price today."
Martin Harrold, Windsor RUFC U15s Forwards Coach.

Lightning Source UK Ltd.
Milton Keynes UK
UKOW012010201112

202509UK00014B/36/P

9 780955 982002